Cletus stood carefully and glanced into the boat. There was a mess of tackle, food, and beer cans lodged in and around the seats. The water rose half the length of the boat, which appeared to have been jammed nose first into the muck at the bottom of the river.

There was no sign of Max or Bill at first. Then he heard Jasper gasp, and he glanced up and followed the line of his friend's gaze to the bank. In the weeds by the bank, an old ball cap bobbed lazily in the water. Beyond that there were a series of deep ruts gouged into the bank. When he followed those ruts up out of the water, and out of sight, Cletus saw what had gotten Jasper's attention. There was a single stained boot lying in the muck, half buried, as if something large had rolled over the top of it. Protruding from the boot about six inches was what was left of a man's leg.

This book is dedicated to the memory of Al Seidel,
Adventurer, Collector, seeker of truth.
The one man I would want with me if I was hunting a dinosaur.

Mystique Press is an imprint of Crosroad Press.

First edition

CROCKATIEL

David Niall Wilson

About the O. C. L. T. Series

There are incidents and emergencies in the world that defy logical explanation, events that could be defined as supernatural, extra-terrestrial, or simply otherworldly. Standard laws do not allow for such instances, nor are most officials or authorities trained to handle them. In recognition of these facts, one organization has been created that can. Assembled by a loose international coalition, their mission is to deal with these situations using diplomacy, guile, force, and strategy as necessary. They shield the rest of the world from their own actions, and clean up the messes left in their wake. They are our protection, our guide, our sword, and our voice, all rolled into one.

They are O.C.L.T.

TALES OF THE O. C. L. T.

AVAILABLE NOW:

Brought to Light: An O.C.L.T. Novella by Aaron Rosenberg
The Temple of Camazotz: An O.C.L.T. Novella by David Niall Wilson
The Parting: An O.C.L.T. Novel by David Niall Wilson
Lost Things by Melissa Scott & Jo Graham
Digging Deep: An O.C.L.T. Novel by Aaron Rosenberg

UPCOMING:

The Highjump: An O.C.L.T. Novel by David McIntee
Schrodinger's Tomb: An O.C.L.T. Novel by David Niall Wilson

OTHER BOOKS BY DAVID NIALL WILSON

NOVELS:
Nevermore, a Novel of Love, Loss, & Edgar Allan Poe
Ancient Eyes
Deep Blue
Killer Green
Sins of the Flash
The Orffyreus Wheel
Darkness Falling
The Mote in Andrea's Eye
On the Third Day
The Second Veil
The Parting: An O.C.L.T. Novel
The Not Quite Right Reverend Cletus J. Diggs & The Crazy Case of Foreman James
Stargate Atlantis: SGA-15: Brimstone (With Patricia Lee Macomber)

THE DECHANCE CHRONICLES:
Heart of a Dragon
Vintage Soul
My Soul to Keep: The Origin of Donovan DeChance
Kali's Tale

NOVELLAS:
Roll Them Bones
The Preacher's Marsh
The Not Quite Right Reverend Cletus J. Diggs & The Currently Accepted Habits of Nature
'Scuse Me, While I Kiss the Sky
Cockroach Suckers
The Temple of Camazotz

COLLECTIONS:
The Fall of the House of Escher & Other Illusions
Defining Moments
A Taste of Blood & Roses
Spinning Webs & Telling Lies

Acknowledgments

This book would not have happened without my daughter's and my love of bad SyFy channel movies. It started as nothing more than a title, a game of putting the names of two creatures together into one to see what would make a good movie title. Since our two birds, who have since moved to a bigger home with a lot of other birds, were cockatiels, and we live near the Great Dismal Swamp, *Crockatiel* was too good to miss. This is—then—a tribute to one heck of a cool bird, Tiki Kowalski, and his buddy Gypsy.

I'd also like to thank Sue Seidel, for agreeing that including Al Seidel as a character in this book was a fitting tribute to an amazing man. Also included are Steve Hislop, Len McMullan, Chuck Gainey, and John Siemens. Crossroad Press fans will note the presence of one "Eddy Dodd" in the prologue of the novel…I bet you can figure out who that is.

I'd also like to thank the love of my life Patricia Lee Macomber for putting up with me laughing and chuckling through the writing of this book. She's tolerated *Sharknado* and *Sharknado 2*—not to mention an endless stream of giant drug-enhanced snakes, ancient artifacts, and unlikely storms on the TV—all contributing to this.

And thank you to North Carolina for providing the setting and the basis for so many memorable characters. Cletus J. Diggs is definitely a native son…

Prologue

2004

The heat surrounded Eddie Dodd like a second skin. It drew the moisture out of him, and the mosquitoes to him with relentless indifference, lending weight to the heavy silence. That silence was what tipped him off, just in time, to pull back into the trees and off the path. The jungle was never silent, and when it was, there was a reason.

Nature has a pecking order. Big eats small, fast eats slow. When the small, large, fast and slow are all quiet, it's a matter of survival. Despite the rifle slung over his back and the 9mm strapped to his hip, Eddie chose that moment to become one with nature... and he waited.

He had only two more days to get through, half-a-dozen samples to collect, and he could hop a jet back home and chill for a few weeks. The others would be returning to camp, and he knew he should do the same, but something held him still. Not many things could quiet a jungle. In fact, he didn't know of any, though he'd seen a prowling tiger silence a much smaller area, to a much smaller degree. He had never heard so little sound. His breath sounded like a fireplace bellows, and his heart pounded like a drum.

The ground beneath him shivered... and grew still. Then it shook, and moments later he heard the crashing, rending sound of trees being pushed aside. Almost simultaneously, birds burst into flight. Animals erupted around him, a wave of baying, barking, howling life. Eddie stood still as stone.

The tree at his back was thick and old. He was completely

concealed behind it, and despite the crashing sounds, he thought anything less than a bulldozer was going to have a hard time shaking it, let alone knocking it down. He considered closing his eyes and just waiting until the jungle returned to its normal cacophony, but couldn't quite bring himself to do it. He was frightened, but he was also curious.

On the far side of the tree, something was moving hard and fast on the trail, something heavy enough to shake the ground. He caught the scent of the river—rotting vegetation and mud— but he had no time to dwell on this. A scream broke the silence with the force of a rushing train. Eddie clapped his hands to his ears, bent double, and pressed back into the tree so hard he felt as if he might leave an impression in the bark.

He couldn't think. He'd never experienced terror of such magnitude. He'd heard things described as blood-chilling, but had never understood, had never realized, just how real that biting cold could be until it paralyzed him in that forest, thousands of miles from home.

He heard hot, heaving breath. Whatever it was, it was big. Very big. He sensed it pausing on the path, and this time he did hold his breath. He wanted to look. He knew it was the worst thing he could do, the thing that could end him, and yet, he needed to know what was out there, what could make a sound like he'd heard. He stood immobile, fighting his instincts; then the tiger screamed.

It was a primal sound, a warning, and a challenge. There was a second, smaller crashing through the brush, and then an answering roar. Eddie heard a great shifting. Something slammed into the trees to his left, and an answering roar rose. He couldn't stand it.

Keeping very low, hugging the tree tightly, he leaned around the edge.

What met his gaze defied belief. A tiger, claws digging in deep, clung to the long, scaled neck of—what? A dinosaur? It looked something like a crocodile, but so much bigger that any comparison was comical. The neck ended in a long snout and jaws lined with vicious, curved teeth.

"Holy shit," Eddie said.

The tiger was not giving ground. It clung tightly, driving its fangs deep into flesh and digging at the thing's neck and shoulders with its huge back claws. The beast whipped its head back and forth like a trapped serpent, but the big cat had it and was not letting go.

Rearing up, the creature lurched, driving back into the trees, trying to rip the tiger loose. At first it seemed as if it wouldn't work, and then, sensing that it was about to be slammed into a thick trunk, the big cat released and sprang free. It launched from the giant reptile's back with a great driving kick and disappeared into the shadows.

Unable to right itself in time, the creature slammed into the jungle. Its tail whipped around and crashed into the solid trunk of the tree behind which Eddie stood, petrified. It missed him by less than a foot, sending a spray of blood and scales and bark down to shower over him. He let it all come, covering him in bark and leaves and gore, and did not move.

Then the thing was up, shaking its snout in rage and pain. It screamed again, and Eddie couldn't even find the strength to cover his ears. He pressed back into the tree, dripping with blood, dirt and sweat, half afraid he'd wet his pants and not caring.

It turned, then. Without a glance in his direction, it crashed off through the brush, ignoring the path, bending large trees out of its way and clambering over and around others... and it was gone.

Eddie listened, but there was nothing. That—thing—and the tiger, were gone. He still couldn't move. He was having difficulty breathing.

"What the hell," he said softly, using the sound of his voice to return himself to reality, "was that?"

He crept around the tree and stared at the trail. There were huge gouges in the dirt where the creature's claws had gripped, branches and leaves littered the ground, and all of it was splattered liberally with blood. He stepped into the open and stopped to listen. He heard nothing. The silence did not comfort him. Silence was what had ushered the thing into his reality in the first place.

He made a quick circuit of the cleared space, and found that several large strips of skin had been torn from the injured beast's wounds. It was scaled. He dropped to one knee and looked more closely. It wasn't like anything 'he'd seen before, exactly, but his first impression was still the strongest. It had looked like the biggest damned crocodile in the world. Then, unable to reconcile the images, he shook his head.

He knew what he'd seen. The beast hadn't walked upright, exactly, but it had been able to rise up, to move on only its hind legs. He tried to focus his memory on the image of it, the shape, the way it had moved, but found his thoughts were muddied. He could only remember snapshots—the tiger, the scream—they were clear.

He glanced down at the slice of skin and made his decision. He wasn't coming back to this jungle again, and he needed a crocodile sample to get out. Damned if he cared if it was some mutant crocodile that ran around on its back feet fighting tigers, he was going home. He knew he couldn't tell anyone what he'd found. No one would believe him, and if they did believe, then they would want to come back—try to find the creature, to hunt it. They would want him along as guide, and, though he'd never considered himself a coward, he knew he'd never be able to do it. The creature's scream still echoed in the back of his mind.

He retrieved his pack and set to work. Moments later, samples secured, he rose and started back down the path. At first, he tried to be stealthy, but every sound, every movement brought back images of the creature, and of the tiger, and before he'd gone twenty yards he'd broken into a trot, and then a flat run. He didn't stop until he'd reached his small boat and pointed it out and away from the bank. He only hoped he could calm himself before he reached camp, turn in his samples, and avoid questions. He doubted if he'd sleep until he was on a plane, and out of Brazil, but it would only be one more day. He had enough samples, as long as the others had been as successful. They'd break camp in the morning, and be back in civilization a few hours later.

As he pulled away from the bank, he heard a sound in the distance. He couldn't be certain, but he thought it was an impossibly loud, wailing scream. He gunned the engine and did not look back.

PART ONE

OLD MILL, NC
2004

1

"**There's something weird as hell about this sample, Sammy.**"

Samuel turned, glaring across the small laboratory in irritation. He was a busy man, and he hated interruptions. His work was important, and he was on a timetable. His funding wasn't going to last forever, and he had no intention of returning to his former position as a lab assistant.

Just short of thirty years, thin and beak-nosed, Samuel Montgomery did not cut an imposing figure. To top it off, he drank so much coffee that he was twitchy. His gaze shifted around the room so quickly at times that people said he reminded them of a squirrel on crack. All of this was heightened when he became annoyed.

"What could possibly," he said slowly, "be weird about a DNA sample from a simple crocodile?" he said. "We have vials of similar cells. I could run a slide projector and display them on the walls like a psychedelic 1960s dance party, and none of them—not one— would be in any way remarkable without the accompanying LSD."

Beatrice dropped her glasses to the end of her nose and glared back at him. She was tall, slender but a little more muscular than she was pretty, with wide shoulders and stringy blonde hair tied off in tight pig-tails. For a horrifying second, despite the imminent danger of contaminating the specimen she was working with, Samuel thought she would pop her gum. She did not.

"You know," she said, "I've seen all of those samples. Before you could set up a slide projector, I could draw the damn things on the wall. I know what crocodile DNA looks like."

Samuel waited.

"This," she said at last, flipping her thumb over to point at the bench to her right, "is weird. It *think* it's crocodile DNA, but I also think there's something wrong with it. What I'm seeing makes no sense, so, if you could haul your skinny butt over here and look at it, I'd be *most* appreciative."

Samuel slid off his stool and stepped back carefully from his microscope. His own sample would remain viable for another thirty minutes, and he was nearly finished. He stepped up to his bench, carefully annotated his last actions, then turned and crossed to Beatrice's workstation. As his irritation faded, his curiosity took over. She was an odd duck, keeping strange hours and only working with him because she couldn't handle "steppin' and carryin' for the man," in a bigger lab, but she was sharp. Weird was a word she used indiscriminately, though, and could mean anything from a small contamination to a completely new species without enough inflection in her voice to provide a warning.

She slid aside, and Samuel bent to the microscope. He adjusted the focus and stared. Then, very slowly and carefully, he adjusted it again. He didn't move for a long moment, and when he did, it was very slowly.

"What the hell," he said, "is that?"

"You tell me, Einstein. It came in that last cooler from South America. It's marked 'crocodile,' and, as I'm sure you noticed, it's *sort* of like a crocodile, but…"

"But it's not," he finished. "Damn. I know I've seen something similar to that, but I can't for the life of me remember where. It's like, a mutation, or …"

"Don't go all *Jurassic Park* on me, Sammy." Beatrice said, grinning.

Samuel glanced at her and caught the expression. He noted, not for the first time, that it transformed her normally cynical, scowling features into something much more intriguing.

"Don't call me Sammy. Sammy sounds like some down-and-out beatnik or a kid with a paper route."

Beatrice didn't reply. She also didn't look apologetic.

"So?" she prodded.

Samuel pressed his eye back to the microscope and tried to clear his thoughts. He didn't have a photographic memory, but he was close to it. What he had was more like a mental filing cabinet. He could access things given peace—and a little time. This was harder, because he knew Beatrice was watching, and he loved it when he managed to surprise her. Most of the time, he knew, he was a crabby, boring-as-hell academic.

Also, there was this sample. Something about it itched at his memory like a stuck record. He had *seen* something like it before...

Then he stood, pushed back from the bench, and shook his head.

"What?" she asked. When he didn't immediately answer she repeated it, smacking him on the shoulder. "What?"

"I think..." he hesitated, and then blurted it out, "I'm afraid I can't do as you ask," he said. "I'm afraid I am going to have to go 'Jurassic' on you...or at least, 'Cretaceous'. I *have* seen this before. It's a crocodile all right, a very old one. I knew it was familiar, but now I remember from where. It was a simulation of Sarcosuchus DNA."

"Sarco what?" Beatrice asked, frowning. "What the hell are you babbling about?"

"Dinosaurs," he said. "Sarcosuchus was an ancestor of the modern croc... sort of like a smaller version of a T-Rex with a long snout, built low to the ground."

Beatrice stared at him.

"So," she said slowly, "you saw a simulation of something very old, and now, after a couple of moments of contemplation, you've decided that the DNA sample under my microscope is, what, a few million years old?"

"No, of course not," Samuel said, distracted. "At least 100 million, probably a bit more. Early Cretaceous Period, if memory serves... it pretty much always does."

"And so," Beatrice continued, "somewhere down in Brazil, there's a dinosaur running around loose? That's what you think?"

"It has nothing at all to do with what I think, does it?" he snapped. "It's not like I slipped it to you, or made it in my basement. It's right there on the slide, and I'm telling you, I know what it is. Remains of Sarcosuchus have been found in Africa, and in parts of South America."

"Let me guess," Beatrice sighed. "Brazil?"

Samuel nodded.

They both stared at the microscope as if it might hop off the bench and chase them around the room.

"Well, hell," Beatrice said at last. "I guess we won't be using *that* sample."

Samuel turned and stared at her. Then, very slowly, his irritation drained away and he actually smiled. Then, softly at first, growing rapidly in strength, Samuel Montgomery began to laugh. Unable to stop herself, Beatrice joined him. It was a long time before they regained enough control to store the sample and separate the rest of the batch it had come from.

"So who do we tell?" Beatrice asked, as they sealed the refrigerator. "I mean, holy crap, who finds dinosaur cells? Where did they come from? Is there one of these things out there still alive, or is this just some odd genetic throwback—some big king croc that had cells he should not be carrying embedded in his code?"

"All good questions," Samuel said. "The answer to the first, and most important, is no one. If we hand this over to anyone—if we even let it slip that we might have come in contact with it—it will disappear so quickly we'll hardly remember it existed. This is our ticket. We have to guard it, study it—and most importantly, we have to prove it is what I say it is."

"How?" Beatrice asked.

When she saw his grin, she shook her head. "No," she said. "No way. I've seen the movies. You can't be serious…"

"Oh, I am," Samuel said. "Not a fully formed creature, but the cells…they are still fresh. We can grow cultures, study them and learn. We'll have all we need to write the paper that will put us on the map. No more sexing pet birds or tracing the lineage of the local Pekingese."

"Jesus," Beatrice said. "You're serious."

"I am," he said, and nodded. "Very."

"I'm not doing this now," she said. "Not today. I think I need a drink. A very strong drink."

"If you don't mind," Samuel said, still smiling, "I believe I will join you. Tomorrow will be soon enough. We're going to have to knock off the regular work rather quickly to make the time…"

"Enough," she said. "No more. Drinks. Sleep."

Samuel nodded absently, lost in thought.

"I think," he said, "I'm going to be having bourbon. Lots of it."

"I'll see that and make it double," Beatrice said. "Let's lock up and get the hell out of here."

2

"**Will you *please* do something about those damned birds? My** god, do they *ever* shut up?"

Neal smiled, but was careful to conceal the expression behind a cough. Katrina was pissed, and he didn't want to fuel the fire. In the next room, Tiki and Gypsy, their Cockatiels, were screeching and wolf whistling, making sounds like ray guns and cartoon spaceships, and had been doing so for about twenty minutes straight. It was nothing new, but sometimes the pair got out of control, and they were loud. He thanked the gods a last time they hadn't decided on a cockatoo. Those birds could be heard for up to two miles.

"I'll take care of them," he said. He rose and grabbed his guitar, heading into the other room. When he got inside, he closed the door behind him, then opened the cage. The two birds chirped a last couple of times, but all they had wanted was a chance to get out and stretch their wings. Neal bent down, took each on one of his fingers, and transferred them to his shoulders.

Then he sat down at his desk and drew the guitar into his lap. He liked to combine time with the birds and his music. It was a hobby—at one time it might have been more, but he'd chosen other trails. Now he played and sang because he enjoyed it, not really caring what anyone thought.

Gypsy, the more curious of the birds, hopped carefully down his arm and shuffled toward the neck of the guitar.

"No you don't," he said. He took her on his finger again and moved her to the desk, where she began contentedly shredding the top page of the manuscript he'd been editing. It didn't matter. He had it all on the computer. He left the paper out for the dual purposes of keeping the bird busy and providing a shield against droppings. Anyone who has spent any time with birds knows, shit happens. A lot.

Tiki Kowalski, the bigger, bolder bird stayed put. He was happy to perch on Neal's shoulder, and would stay there until he either got bored and took flight to the top of his cage for a snack, or was put away. The only thing he liked better than sitting on Neal's shoulder was courting Gypsy... which was the problem.

Tiki had a very distinctive mating song. The votes were not in yet on whether Gypsy was even a female. They'd searched websites and found inconsistent "rules" for sexing birds, but nothing conclusive. They'd even taken a feather that came loose when Gypsy took a wild flight around the house, escaping her room and panicking in the larger space beyond. She'd hit a wall, and Neal had caught her, like a basket catch by Willie Mays. The feather, collateral damage, he'd snagged and bagged. He already had a similar feather from Tiki, just in case his mating virtuosity was that of a female seeking a mate.

The one sure way to sex a pet bird is to send off a DNA sample for analysis. Not horribly expensive, but you needed a sample—a blood feather was perfect. He'd been hoping to prove that Gypsy was a girl, and Tiki was absolutely a male. They didn't want baby birds, but there seemed no real danger of that. Gypsy, while not exactly rejecting Tiki's advances, was certainly never in an amorous mood. Tiki was not fazed—he had developed a song and a dance. The family called it the *Tiki Tango*, and once he got going, he was a force of nature. Almost nothing could stop him until the song had run its course. Gypsy had learned to mimic the song, but it wasn't quite the same. Neal had even made the irritating ditty his ring tone for a while, resulting in some odd looks at business meetings.

He turned his attention to the guitar. He'd been trying to perfect a favorite song by Passenger, he thought it was titled "'Let her go," but wasn't sure. For some reason the lyrics of the simple chorus kept jumbling in his head. It didn't help that Tiki started almost immediately picking at the chain that held the lucky penny around his neck, pulling and digging in with his not insubstantial claws.

After a few runs through the song, Neal set the guitar aside and took Tiki on his finger.

"Asshole," he said. "I was about to get it."

Tiki tilted his head to one side and reached out, gripping Neal's glasses and tugging playfully. Gypsy, meanwhile, had grown bored with the paper, and the desk, and hopped to Neal's arm. When Tiki noticed, he sidled slowly over, and Neal couldn't help laughing.

"No you don't, pal," he said. "Mommy is already pissed off at you and your big mouth. No *Tiki Tango* for you today. I'll get you two some millet and you can get back in that cage. I'm closing the door, and *you* are going to shut up, if you know what's good for you."

He carried them back to their cage, filled their food dishes with seeds and pulled their millet holder out. They loved the stuff. Kat called it "crack" for Cockatiels. It came in long, branch-like "sprays" that he tucked into a plastic tube and hung from the disco-ball toy in the center of their cage. He knew it would be decimated by the next day, but it would also, mostly, keep them quiet.

He grabbed his guitar and left the room, closing the door behind him to block the sound in case the millet failed in its mission. Kat really loved the birds, but when they got noisy, they could try the patience of a saint.

He carefully tucked the Martin back into its case, smiling as he did so. He'd worked a lifetime to own an instrument like this. He probably should still have waited, but Kat had insisted he go ahead and get it. It was one of those special things that could always make him smile. The birds were like that too, and the dogs, and the cats, and all the other animals that had made their way through the zoo they called a house.

Most of their kids had moved on to lives of their own. Their youngest, Mary, was ten, and loved the animals like they did. All their lives they had lived with the certain knowledge that there had to be a secret symbol on the outside of their house that said

"Suckers live here" in cat, dog, and several other animal languages. Nothing else could explain the menagerie.

He closed the guitar case and headed to the kitchen for a drink. Kat was checking on the crockpot full of chili, and Neal's mouth watered as he came up behind her, wrapping her in a hug. He'd also waited a lifetime for the chance to spend the rest of that same life with someone who cared—someone who actually loved him, probably more than he deserved. She also made a mean pot of chili.

"I'm going to move them out into the garage," she said.

He knew she didn't mean it, but he wished that the animals would listen. Not for the first time, he thought the perfect super power would be the ability to communicate with them. Flying would be cool, super strength would come in useful, but how much could you learn and know if you understood what the birds and wolves, bears and bulls, and goddam Cockatiels, for that matter, were thinking and saying? At least he might convince Tiki not to crap on Kat's shoulder...

"They're settled down," he said. "I think Tiki is getting a little amorous... must be in the air." He kissed her on the neck.

She turned and raised an eyebrow. "As far as we know, Tiki and Gypsy are both boys, and all he's going to get is pecked on the head."

"We'll know soon," Neal said.

Kat shook her head.

"I can't believe you sent them a feather. Really? All the things you could worry over, and you choose sexing a Cockatiel."

"You're just afraid Gypsy *will* be a girl. Then you'll know when Tiki sits on your shoulder and 'chirps the bird,' he's serious."

"You're a jerk."

"But you love me."

She leaned back into him and laughed. In the other room, Tiki started singing again, and Neal laughed too.

"Is it working for you?" he asked.

She turned and whacked him on the arm.

"I *hate* the bird," she said. She was still laughing.

"I know," he said. "I know. He hates you too, but it's a love/hate thing."

Without warning, he scooped her up in his arms and carried her to the bedroom. Before they got inside, he lifted his head and started whistling, mocking Tiki's song.

"You want to survive," she said, kissing him, "you'll quit while you're behind."

He laughed again and kicked the door closed behind them. They had about an hour before their daughter would return home, and he didn't want to waste it. There were far too few times when they were alone. Faintly, he could still hear Tiki singing, but he held the laugh. No sense spoiling a perfect moment.

3

Samuel sat in the lab, staring at a set of cultures, a tray of test tubes and the clock. He had been working steadily for fourteen hours. Beatrice had gone out for sushi and left him to finish up, but he couldn't bring himself to finalize the day's work. It was so important, so momentous, that the thought of closing it down and moving into a seemingly endless period of waiting maddened him.

As it turned out, they'd had enough of the sample to set up three separate cultures. They had agreed to try with the first and preserve the others so that, on the chance they succeeded and something amazing actually happened—a thing they both believed likely but could not bring themselves to count on—they would have proof to back up their work and something for the inevitable follow-on doubters to use in recreating their results. The important thing was that they were first to the table, well-documented, and credited for the work.

Samuel had spent a long life being so detail conscious he'd been called anal on more than one occasion and actually examined during his childhood to be certain his desire to color code his socks and arrange his toys by size, shape, and the year he'd received them on his shelves was not severe OCD. He just didn't believe in disorganization. It was a trait that had served him well in this small lab, and less well in larger corporations where he didn't have the authority to arrange things the way he liked them. He realized it was a strength as well as a problem, but it wasn't something he could control, and his efforts to cover for himself always seemed to come off as arrogance.

Here, he was free to keep things any way he liked them. Beatrice didn't share his need for organization, but she appreciated it, and she stayed out of his way. He realized it made her life easier, and he often took this out on her by being grumpy, but they were a good team, and this—this pile of glass and cells and chemicals on the bench in front of him—was their ticket.

Genetics was a field where you could still make a name for yourself. Regardless of what people were led to believe, things like cloning, organ growth, genetic body modification, were not as illegal as the government let on. In fact, there were dozens of think tanks, laboratories, and long-term experiments going on behind the scenes at any given moment—some of them so far out there that even Samuel had a hard time wrapping his head around them.

The thing was that those big programs were littered with genius and ego. One, maybe two people would be remembered on the scene of any true breakthrough, and a lot of the programs the government backed were likely to achieve results one might *not* want their name associated with, once they finally went public.

This was different. This was the Holy Grail. While science had a good-sized public-interest factor, and some scientists could actually be considered pop icons—it was a serious crapshoot finding something the public cared about long-term enough to sustain viability. If he and Beatrice managed to go *Jurassic Park* on the world, actually brought a viable dinosaur to life and presented it to the scientific community, that was the key to an amazing future. Movies would be made. Bad SyFy movies would abound.

He glanced at the materials he was working with, picked up the card for the subject identification and laughed. Dinosaurs and birds were so closely related that at times they could be considered evolutionary pairs. Knowing this, and having limited resources, they had shuffled through the samples they had available, and they'd come across a pair of blood feathers, sent in by their owners for sexing. Birds were notoriously hard to pin down without DNA or the actual appearance of fertilized eggs—they represented a large part of the lab's daytime business—and these feathers had both come from a single household, a pair of Cockatiels.

Beatrice had objected at first. Sarcosuchus was a crocodile. A damn big one, but still, a creature that had basically changed very little over the centuries. On the surface, the connection to birds that was all the rage with T-Rexes and other dinosaurs didn't seem to apply. The reality, however, is that crocodiles and birds are more closely associated than most other reptilian creatures could claim, so the DNA link was not as far-fetched as it seemed.

The birds, Tiki Kowalski and Gypsy, bore similar markings. The note that had accompanied the feathers explained that Tiki was aggressive sexually, and it was unclear how Gypsy was reacting. Samuel had seen similar notes a thousand times. Birds were intriguing creatures—he had a very chatty Conure named Livingston that had been his companion for nearly a decade. He'd thought of getting the bird a partner, but, and he was aware how sad the notion was, he was worried that if he did he'd lose time with one of his only friends.

They had sexed the birds, and mailed off the results. Tiki was definitely a male. The slightly less cheerful news was that Gypsy was also a male. The two were friends, but apparently Mr. Tiki Kowalski was one frustrated bird. He hoped the owners would find a way to deal with it, but all he cared about at the moment was that Tiki's cells—culled from the feather—had blended nicely with those of the sample that had come in from Brazil. He wasn't certain what they would end up with when all was said and done, but they'd both agreed that trying for a male—whatever—was safer than having a female that might escape and find a way to mate. After the lesson of Spielberg's films, frog DNA was out of the question. No Cockatiel in either of their memories had suddenly changed sex, as amphibians had been known to. Silly to base fears on fiction, but too much of the science they took for granted had its roots in stories and novels. Besides, what they had done had worked.

They might have been able to clone from just the sample, but it was foreign to anything they were familiar with, and the bonding of the DNA made the work simpler. They could also have used cells from a regular crocodile, but were afraid the result might prove less than exciting. What if it was just a mutation, and when bonded to DNA from a normal creature, just normalized itself and they ended up with an unremarkable crocodile and a lot of wasted time?

So Cockatiels it was. The irony wasn't lost on him. What they were making—what they would bring to life—the breeders who created Schnoodles and Puggles would probably call a damned "Crockatiel"—and he found that he didn't care. As long as it made him famous—as long as he and Beatrice got the credit and something came of it.

"Crockatiel it is," he said softly. "Rise! Live!" He laughed softly.

Then he noticed the sudden pounding of rain, and vaguely, as if the sound was fading in from a distance, he became aware of wind roaring outside. He hadn't known it was going to storm. It would suck driving the crooked road back to town, and he wondered where in hell Beatrice had gotten to.

Outside the lab, the wind had kicked up to nearly fifty miles per hour. The tops of the trees lining the road leading in from the highway had begun to sway, dipping even lower at the press of stronger gusts. The rain, which had started at about the strength of a heavy shower, pounded onto the windshield of Beatrice's Jeep. She fought to keep it on the road, and cursed under her breath.

It wasn't the first time that she and Samuel had managed to overlook things going on in the world around them. They lived insular lives, and they were both focused on their work. Currently that work was fascinating beyond anything she'd ever been involved in, and she'd done little but sleep, rise, eat, work, eat and repeat since they started. She doubted Samuel had taken a single full night to sleep, and was absolutely certain he'd not wasted any time on the news.

Still, managing not to notice the hourly warnings of an oncoming hurricane for nearly two days was a new high—or low—even for them. She'd gotten their food as the restaurant was closing. Early. When she'd asked why, the girl had looked at her like she was crazy and explained about the storm.

"Hurricane Callie is hovering off the North Carolina coast," the radio crackled. "Current radar tracking projects it will cut inland across the Outer Banks and skirt the coast past Hampton Roads before moving north. Callie is a Category Two storm, but projected to grow in strength before landfall. Evacuations are in effect for…"

There was no evacuation in effect where the lab was located, but it was directly in the path of the storm. There was just time for her to get out there, get Samuel, and get out. Despite the danger, Beatrice was thinking of the samples, and the cultures they were processing. She hoped she could convince Samuel to go, but common sense and genius aren't particularly dependent on one another, and she knew it would be a struggle.

She was frightened. She'd been through storms in her hometown, back in Illinois, huge dark thunderstorms and tornadoes that ripped through towns and obliterated everything in their path. It wasn't the same, but she'd spent enough time obsessively viewing footage of hurricanes since moving to North Carolina to have developed a respect bordering on paranoia about them. It didn't help that every time the wind blew hard enough to move a leaf, the local weather men began predicting doom and destruction, or that you could pick up your hurricane survival checklist at any grocery or convenience store.

Beatrice wasn't scared of much. The local rednecks had tried pushing her, courting her, and come up wanting (and hurting, in several instances). Insults to her lifestyle, dress code (or lack thereof) and lack of a social life flowed over her like water. She had long since come to the conclusion that surrounding herself with the things she enjoyed was the only sensible way to live, and that if life sent someone along that happened to be comfortable there—that was great. If not, at least no time would be wasted chasing things she didn't care about, or living up to the expectations of a world that, for the most part, didn't interest her.

This was different. The windshield wipers were having trouble parting the pouring rain long enough to give her a clear view of the road. By the time the lab came into sight, she was almost on top of it. She slowed, wheeled into the parking lot, and pulled to a stop as close to the front door as possible. She glanced at her umbrella, and then realized how quickly it would be destroyed. Instead, she wrapped herself around the box of sushi, leapt out of the Jeep, slammed the door behind her and ran in crazy, splashing strides. Thankfully, Samuel must have been watching for her; he opened the door as she hit the small concrete porch, and she nearly dove inside. He closed the door quickly and stood, blinking and staring.

"What?" she said.

"Nothing," Samuel said. He failed to hide his grin. "You're… wet."

She stared at him. She would have laughed, but her teeth were chattering suddenly, and the wind whipping against the walls and through the trees had begun to sound like the roar of a large train.

"It's a hurricane," she said. "Hurricane Callie. We didn't know… we have to go…"

"Too late, I'm afraid," he said, almost cheerfully.

She stared at him, trying to figure out whether he was stupid, or just hadn't heard her correctly.

"We have to *go!*" she said.

He grabbed her by the shoulders and steadied her.

"We can't get out of here now," he said. "The winds are too strong. The storm will be here in less than half an hour, and the outer edges are already here. There is nowhere we could drive to that is safer than here, and there is no way we'd make it if we tried. The road will probably flood, but we're on higher ground. We're in this for the long haul, so I need you to calm down and listen."

"But…"

"No buts. I've lived here all my life. I've survived a few of these storms in my time, and I know what I'm doing. Do you know why I chose this building for the lab?"

Beatrice, feeling shell-shocked, bit her lip and shook her head.

"It was built by the Jamieson-Wicks Corporation. They are based right here in North Carolina. Andrea Wicks, the founder? She's probably the world's foremost expert on hurricanes. They say she nearly stopped one once, but that's not important. What *is* important is that this building is one of her prototypes. It was designed to withstand winds of up to two hundred miles an hour.

It has a small generator that runs on propane for up to a week, and I had the tanks filled a while back. The best part? Everyone thought she was crazy. No one bought the buildings, no one bought the technology—at least not below the large, corporate level—and even though I'm pretty sure she and her Navy pilot husband had something to do with Hurricane Andrea, a few years back, only being a little over a Category One when it hit, you don't see people out there trying to stop this one."

"So, you're trusting a crazy woman?" Beatrice asked.

"I trust you, but that's not the point. The point is, in all of this area, there are only a dozen or so buildings as safe as this one during a hurricane, and she built all of them. I got it for a song. The previous owners didn't see the design as a selling point, but I know what I know. We'll be fine."

"What about food?"

Samuel eyed the bag she carried.

"We seem to be covered for this evening," he said. "If we have to stay, we'll be fine. I'm not really much of a survivalist, but this place inspired me. I couldn't help stocking the emergency locker. We have lights, batteries, a radio and a small television set, in case we lose the Internet. We have canned goods, and even some old C-rations I picked up at the Army Navy store up in Virginia."

Beatrice dropped her fists to her hips and frowned at him.

"Where has all of this been?" she asked.

"What do you mean?"

"This!" she said, waving toward the back of the building. "This… normal person preparedness crap. I've known you what, three years now? Not once have you shown the slightest interest in anything but the lab, the work, an occasional beer. Now I find out you're a closet hurricane freak of some kind, you actually *prepare* for things that don't involve microscopes, and the thought of hundred-mile-an-hour winds doesn't even faze you. Who the hell *are* you?"

Samuel laughed.

"I told you, I've lived here all my life. Some of that time occurred prior to college, you know. I've always been fascinated by storms.

I've seen what they can do, and I respect it. That's why I wanted this building. Andrea Jamieson-Wicks is a personal hero of mine. Can't I have secrets?"

Just then the wind picked up, and the lights wavered, then steadied. Beatrice turned and stared at the window, as if she expected it to implode at any moment.

"While we're questioning things," Samuel said, "what happened to the not-scared-of-anything bitch-chick I hired? It's just some wind and rain…"

"It's wind and rain that could flood the roads, knock down trees, and drown a city," she said simply. "I don't like thunder—I don't like rain. I know, most 'spooky' chicks who wear black and scowl a lot are into dark and stormy nights…not this one. I wish I was a million miles from here…"

"We'll be fine," Samuel repeated. "While we've got Internet, let me show you some things…might not make you feel better, but it might, and it will certainly pass the time better than watching that window…"

4

NOAA radar tracked the storm as, rather than bouncing off the Outer Banks of North Carolina the way most hurricanes did, it turned and drove inland. It was still a Category Three storm. Cutting across land weakened it, but only slightly. Northeastern North Carolina called for an almost complete evacuation as driving rain raised water levels and roaring wind drove the rain across the state with relentless fury.

Roads were already blocked by fallen trees, and power was going down in large blocks as poles were toppled and lines were torn free of transformers. Small pockets of civilization held their ground. The highways leading west and south were clogged with fleeing families trying to get far enough out of the storm's path to survive and live to return.

Samuel's lab, as he'd expected, stood fast. The generators hummed, the lights remained lit, the roof did not leak, and, though isolated, he and Beatrice were safe. Before the clouds obscured their satellite and cut off the Internet signal, he showed her records of the Jamieson-Wicks Foundation, their fabled battle with Hurricane Andrea, and even the designs they'd made public for pumps that could, if properly placed, weaken a huge storm and save lives.

In the end, it was too much for science, and even the government. The documentation of what they'd done was too scattered, and with wars in the middle east, there was no funding for any new version of the 1960s "Storm Fury" project. The idea of fighting hurricanes was considered antiquated—like Area 51 flying saucers and mind control. Something that tax dollars had been thrown at and wasted.

The building designs had been adopted in many countries overseas, particularly in Japan, and the company was solvent, but there had been no more reports of battles with big storms. None of that was the point. Sensing her fear, Samuel had managed to find records of the building they were trapped in—diagrams and data substantiating the design. It was meant to withstand up to a Category Four storm. So far, though any warranty was certainly expired, it was succeeding marvelously.

"So, we're basically trapped here until things blow over?" Beatrice said.

"Trapped—or protected. It depends on how you look at it, doesn't it? I suspect it will be longer than that, though. If the storm is as bad as they say it is, roads are going to be closed to traffic for days, maybe weeks. We have power, and if we're careful with it we have enough fuel to last until the sun returns. At that point, unless the panels have been ripped off the roof, we'll be able to charge the solar batteries, and hold out even longer…"

"What about our samples?" Beatrice asked. "If we lose power, they'll be spoiled. The cultures as well. Possibly the most important discovery in –ever– could be lost to time, and you and I will be back to sexing birds for bored housewives. Is there anything we can do?"

"We can continue to work, after a fashion," Samuel said. "We can record what we are doing very, very carefully, capture images of the DNA, document what we find, and hope that we are thorough and careful enough that, even if everything is lost, someone will see that we could not have made it all up. Somewhere out there is a man, or woman, who already knows what we discovered. Some-one sent us that sample, and it's possible, with time and a bit of luck, that we'll figure out who they are. We're not letting this go. I scanned the information from that sample label so we can try to trace it back.

"In the meantime, we pray that the generators don't fail. We can take some of the cultures and seal them. We have the equipment to keep them viable for some time, even if the power fails. It's all a game of hours and minutes now."

Beatrice nodded. As the wind continued to fail in its efforts to blow them up and over the rainbow, she regained her composure. She wanted to get a glimpse outside, to see if her car was still there, or if trees blocked the road, but much more than that she did *not* want to open *anything*. It was better to hear the roar, and the distant crash of huge things falling, but to not be a part of it. When it was all over, when the world returned to normal, she could think about things like cars. For now, she needed a focus, and work was as good a distraction as any—better than most.

"How far could we take it?" she asked. "I mean, without any facilities other than what we have, how far could we take one of the cultures? Could we keep one viable? Alive? How long—how mature? It seems to me that, if we could get a single viable organism, we could bring it to a stage of…life?"

"It would survive more easily," Samuel finished her sentence. "It's brilliant. It's the kind of thinking that will ensure our fame and fortune. It's…"

"Time to get started," Beatrice said. "We could lose power at any moment, super-storm proof lab or not. We need to hurry."

Without further words, they set to work. There was a sort of incubator in one of the back storerooms and Samuel dragged it into the main lab. They plugged it in, lit it off, and he actually laughed when it hummed to life without a glitch.

"I'll get this set up," he said. "Get one of the cultures, and get some control readings. We'll monitor it carefully, and if it appears to be maturing, we'll move it to the incubator."

Beatrice turned and headed for the refrigerated storage. She knew what to do, and it gave her something to focus on. She'd been trained for this, studied for a moment like this all of her life.

They weren't really fully equipped for what they intended to do. Some of the equipment would have to be modified or flat out invented. It wasn't out of the question, but it was going to be tricky. It was one thing to keep a DNA sample fresh, and very much another to introduce the necessary elements for a viable embryo.

They had everything they needed, but not because they had ever planned on using it.

They also had a great number of samples on hand. They were the go-to service for a number of exotic animal breeders for sexing of infants, and genetic profiling of hybrids. They not only had cultures from a number of birds on hand, but they had fertile eggs from a number of species as well. They could imprint the DNA that Samuel had bonded with the Cockatiel on the fertile egg of a bird. They would have to try a number of times, possibly dozens, to get it right, but for the moment, all they had was time.

It occurred to her more than once as she worked that they might be overstepping some unseen, unspoken boundary. While it was true that genetic manipulation had become almost a way of life for a great body of scientists, none of them had yet faced a situation quite like this one. There were groups fighting to revive extinct species, but those were recent extinctions. Even the group trying to clone a wooly mammoth was looking at only a few thousand years. This was reaching back through an eerie, mail-order time machine to a world that no longer existed. Also, there was the not insignificant fact that the sample they had received was recent. It wasn't sucked from the blood of an ancient mosquito, or pulled out of a glacier.

If they succeeded, they were going to be famous and infamous at the same time. If they failed, and told anyone what they had done, they would become the pair who'd found a miracle sample of dinosaur DNA and ruined it playing Frankenstein in the Great Dismal Swamp. Either way, once the wind and rain faded, and the roads were cleared, their lives were going to change forever.

She prepared several Petrie dishes with the proper solutions, and then went to the rear of the building to the refrigerated storage to retrieve eggs. The first she found were Cockatiel, and she pulled them out without really thinking about it. She also grabbed the samples Samuel had prepared. About halfway back to her workstation, she glanced at the label he'd applied, and snorted laughter. For one long moment she stumbled, nearly falling and dropping the whole mess into a puddle of lost potential on the floor.

The label read. "Crockatiel."

5

The storm took nearly a full day to blow over. It bounced in off the coast and caught a freak warm front blowing down from the northwest, then slowed almost to a stop before suddenly weakening and shooting off northward. Samuel and Beatrice dragged out cots, cooked ramen noodles and ate C-Rations from the emergency stores. They worked in shifts, recording their experiment in almost paranoid detail.

They laughed and joked, but once the work began in earnest, they knew they'd cast their lines. They would either come up empty in the biggest opportunity of their lives, or they would soon be rubbing elbows at a higher level.

Beyond the safety of the lab's walls, so much rain had fallen that small rivers and ponds had grown overnight, invading any low spot and seeping deep into the already moist ground near the swamp. The wind had died down, though occasional gusts still tore through.

Near the front door, where the road had stretched off along the edge of the swamp out toward U. S. Route 17, a tangle of fallen trees, debris, mud and other less-identifiable rubble blocked their escape. In the distance, the sound of heavy equipment could be heard as men slunk out of their barns and trailers and the remnants of their homes and set to work clearing away what Mother Nature had flung at them.

Chainsaws roared. Tractors and heavy equipment that hadn't seen the light of day in years went to work, chugging, tugging, and towing trees, broken homes, and flooded vehicles off of the main roads and out of people's driveways and yards. Branches were cut free of crushed roofs, tarpaper and shingles were hung. All of this Samuel and Beatrice were peripherally aware of.

They had the radio, and through some miracle of cabling that no doubt linked back to the original Jamieson-Wicks design for the building, their power and Internet had been restored. They watched videos of heroic rescues, and listened to endless news stories about price-gouging store owners, acts of kindness, and idiotic weathermen who seemed to believe the only way to real "street cred" in their field was to stand fast in the eye of a huge storm and try to talk over the roaring of wind in their microphones.

It was crazy, a little surreal, and even more so because it didn't have any particular effect on them. They were insulated, well fed, warm, and busy. The rest of it was like a bad movie that they couldn't switch channels to escape.

That was inside.

Just outside the lab, things were also happening.

Sometime in the past, several hundred years back, an acorn had fallen into the murky ground. At that time, there were no roads. If men came near, it was on a hunting or fishing trip, and they never stayed. That acorn, as acorns do, took root and sprouted, and the result, over that span of centuries, was one big-assed oak tree. Three men holding hands couldn't have reached around the trunk near its base. It was scarred and weathered. Far up its trunk was a blackened fissure, a lingering kiss from a bolt of lightning during another long-forgotten storm. It held squirrels and bugs, birds and even a Turkey Vulture's nest, near the top.

A little-known thing (mostly because the circumstances necessary just aren't common) is that the roots of an oak tree grow in a huge ball. Despite the immense size of such a tree, this ball of roots doesn't reach as far into the Earth as you might think, and isn't as big as an engineer probably would have designed it. Hurricane-force winds, in conjunction with the softening of the ground due to torrential rain, can work the whole thing loose. Mostly, this happens a little, and the tree settles. The ground dries and hardens, and the roots stretch out a little farther, maintaining balance. Mostly.

The tree just to the rear and about fifty yards to the south of the lab had weathered this process many times. Over the years, it had bowed, swayed, and deflected lightning, but through all that it stood its ground. The upper branches leaned now, in toward the lab, and the tree was very tall. Top heavy and slightly off balance. Imperceptibly, it tilted, very, very slowly. Anyone standing near it would have heard strange sounds from the ground beneath—tearing and snapping, soft slurping sounds, like ropes snapping through slimy mud.

In the end, it was a final gust of wind, not more than fifteen or twenty miles per hour, that became the straw that broke the proverbial camel's back. With a grinding, tearing sound, the tree gave up its grip on the moist earth. Slowly at first, and then more rapidly, the trunk swayed, leaned, and at last—with a roar—dropped.

Samuel heard the creaking groan of the big tree letting go. He didn't really know what the sound was, but something in his memory caused the sound to drive into the nerves of his spine like needles of ice. He turned, saw that Beatrice had lifted her face from the microscope she'd been examining to glance at him. Her look was at once quizzical, and terrified.

"What the…"

She never got the words out. The grinding roar of roots snapping, the earth letting go its long hold on the gigantic oak, the rush of air as the massive trunk and widespread branches dropped, drowned out all sound. There was a moment—a single moment—when time stood still. They locked gazes and stood, petrified. Then, not really even sure why, Samuel moved. He dove for Beatrice, knocked her from her stool, and pulled her down beneath the heavy bench, ducking in beside her and holding her tightly.

There was a snapping crash from the rear of the building. The sound was deafening, a huge booming thud, accentuated by the sound of walls and equipment smashing under the massive weight of the tree. From where they sat, beneath the workbench, they couldn't be certain what was happening. It sounded like an explosion had removed the rear of the lab, but neither of them was inclined to stand and look.

"What…" Beatrice said softly. She didn't finish the question.

When no further sound followed the crash, Samuel extracted himself, slightly embarrassed by how close he'd held her, and stood. He started back toward the source of the sound. Beatrice rose and followed a few steps behind.

When they stepped through the door to the rear of the building, Samuel stopped short. The enormous tree had crushed the side of the building nearest to it, driving its branches through the roof and embedding them in the floor. The basic structure of the building was intact, but the back of the lab—the climate-controlled storage, emergency food supplies, and the generator—were obliterated. Just like that they'd gone from a self-sufficient island to stranded.

Then Samuel lurched forward with a cry.

"What?" Beatrice said. "What is it?"

"The samples," he said. "We have to try and get them…"

He reached the tree and began forcing his way in and through the tangle of branches. Most of those that had penetrated were large, and there was no way he could move them out of the way. He was forced to squirm and wiggle through, all the time trying to pierce the shadows beneath and see how bad the damage had been.

Beatrice watched from the doorway, still not quite brave enough to step into the room. She knew her fear wasn't logical, but she couldn't quite rid herself of the notion that the roof might collapse, or the ruined generator might find just enough remaining energy to explode.

She knew he was right. They had a few cultures in the front of the lab that they might be able to keep viable, with luck. The lack of power was going to make that tough. She turned, realizing they had little time, and hurried back to her workstation. They had containers that would maintain the specimens at a proper temperature, avoiding contamination, but every moment mattered. She needed to transfer what they'd been studying and working on to a safe environment and seal them off.

She worked quickly. In the other room she heard Samuel banging around and cursing, but she blanked him from her mind. The work gave her something to concentrate her fraying nerves on. She still shook slightly from the crash of the tree, and she didn't want to think about others just like it that might be hovering over them like huge sledgehammers ready to strike.

She didn't have much. There were five viable cell samples—two of them were tucked away in the freezer in the back room and buried under a tree. The other three were still on the workbench. She sealed them away as carefully as possible. The cylinder she used was similar to those stored in the refrigeration unit. As she sealed it, she noticed the paperwork that had accompanied the original sample. On impulse, she folded it carefully and tucked it into her pocket. It contained the serial number of the sample and the address of the company that had supplied it. She didn't know what use it might be, but she knew she'd regret it if she lost track. She also tucked away the information for the DNA of the bird they'd used as well.

She was just finishing her cleanup and salvage operation when Samuel staggered out of the back room. He was sweating and frowning, and his breath was heavy.

"It's no use," he said. "I can't get into that unit. There's a huge branch pressed up against it; we'd need a chainsaw to cut it loose. Without power, it's only a matter of time until everything in there is ruined."

"Even when they get back here to us," Beatrice said, "they won't be able to restore power immediately.

Samuel shook his head. "Nope. It might be possible to get a generator in but I'm sure they're all in use. All the preparations I made, and it never occurred to me to add a level of redundancy."

"No way to have anticipated something like this..."

"I know. What were you doing?"

She showed him the canister where she'd sealed their work.

"I think I got enough to salvage this," she said. "We'll need our notes..."

Samuel broke into a grin. He stepped forward, forgetting the dirt and sweat coating his skin, and hugged her.

Beatrice stiffened, just for a second, and then returned the hug.

"You're a genius," he said. "You truly are..."

"Just make sure you remember that when we're giving our Nobel speech," she said.

Samuel let her go and stepped back.

"Well," he said. "I guess I'd better see if I can dig a couple of backpacks out of that mess. We'll need to get moving if we want to find some semblance of civilization before it gets dark, and we're going to have to find someplace with power and a freezer."

"They have freezers at pizza parlors. Just saying..."

Samuel shook his head again and turned away, but she caught his smile as he did so. Even a walk along the edge of a hurricane-torn swamp suddenly didn't seem so bad.

"We'll have to keep this quiet," Samuel said, returning with the packs, half loaded with water bottles and odds and ends he'd gathered from the decimated story area. "We have to secure the specimens, and then we have to find a place to work. I have some money saved, and there will be insurance money..."

"I know a place near Raleigh that rents lab space," Beatrice said.

"Sounds like a plan. First, though, we have to find our way out of here."

They shouldered the packs, and stepped outside. Out of habit, Samuel turned and began locking the door. Then he stopped himself and laughed.

He turned, pocketed the keys, and started walking. Beatrice fell in beside him, and they began the long, laborious trek over and around fallen trees, avoiding places where the water had overrun the road, making their way back to Old Mill. Neither of them looked back.

PART TWO

OLD MILL, NC
2014

6

The Cotton Gin was hopping. It was Saturday night, and the usual mix had flooded the bar: Coast Guard sailors on liberty; farmers quenching the thirst they'd built in the fields; hunters and fishermen either celebrating a successful trip, or planning one for the early morning that would likely be scuttled by too much beer and too little sleep.

Behind the bar, Willow Nixon split her time between fending off the advances of the men lining the counter and pouring endless pitchers and mugs of beer. On one end of the slick, polished counter stood the jukebox, and at the other, behind a dark curtain, a hallway leading to private rooms in the back, and the restrooms.

Cletus J. Diggs sat at that end, nursing his third beer, and wondering if his buddy Jasper was ever going to show up. They'd planned a fishing trip for the next morning, and Jasper was supposed to be checking with some boys who'd gone that morning, hoping for tips on what was biting and where.

It was a ritual Jasper insisted on, even though Cletus knew that, no matter what anyone else said, they would end up at the same old fishing hole where they always went. It was secluded, far enough from town that they could bring a cooler of beer and find their way back without running into any local law enforcement, and it had never failed to provide enough fish for dinner.

Jasper, though, wanted more. He had bought a boat at a local estate auction, and he was determined to launch it in the Perquimans River and head into the swamp. He'd heard tales of monster

catfish, gar as long as a tree, and a number of other unlikely tro-
phies to be had, and he was obsessed with the idea of making one
of them his own.

"It'll be perfect, Cletus," he'd said on the phone. "We'll get the
inside dope on where to anchor, and I'll latch onto one of them
swamp monsters. Then you can take pictures and write me up for
The Weekly Globe, you know, like them farmers with the giant
grasshoppers."

"You are so full of crap your eyes are brown," Cletus had told
him.

It was true, about the eyes *and* the crap. Still, it kept Jasper out
of other kinds of trouble. Cletus was just tipping the pitcher to fill
his glass for the fourth time, promising himself Jasper was split-
ting the tab whether he drank any or not, when his buddy pushed
through the door and crossed over to the bar.

Right off the bat, Cletus knew something was up. Jasper was
moving faster than, well, Jasper. He had a gleam in his eye Cletus
could make out from where he sat, and a grin so wide Cletus knew if
the truck window had been open, his teeth would be sporting bugs.

"You," Jasper said, almost out of breath from the exertion of
rushing in all the way from the parking lot, "are not gonna *believe*
what I heard today. I mean, Cletus…"

Jasper slid onto the barstool beside Cletus and stopped to catch
his breath and pour a glass of beer. It was almost graceful, and Cletus shook his head.

"What the hell are you talkin' about, Jaz?"

Jasper didn't respond immediately. He raised the beer and
drained half of it, holding up a finger dramatically, as if Cletus
might walk away or interrupt him again before he could reveal his
big secret.

After a quick, soul-cleansing burp, Jasper grabbed Cletus by
the forearm and leaned close. "You know ol' Max Nixon? From
over by Hertford?"

Cletus nodded. "You know I do. I stood for his daughter in
court last month when she smacked that no-good boyfriend of
hers on the head with a coffee mug."

Cletus was a man of many talents. One of the hats he often wore was that of common-law lawyer, helping those who could not afford more professional legal counsel.

"Yeah, I forgot about that. Anyway, Max and Bill White was out on the river last night. They took that big boat of Bill's on down the river toward the swamp. They was pullin' in some catfish and washing away their worries with cold beer when they saw it."

Cletus stared. He waited. Then, patiently, he asked.

"Saw what, Jaz?"

Jasper leaned in even closer. "A goddamned *dinosaur* Cletus. No shit. They said it looked like a crocodile, but the damned head rose up out of the water higher than a man's head. Said if they hadn't gotten the motor on that boat in reverse, they'd have been sunk. Said it ate a damned *deer!*"

Cletus blinked. He sat back, picked up his beer, and stared at it for several breaths before turning to face his friend.

"You have *got* to be kidding me."

Jasper shook his head. He was ready to launch into a more detailed discourse, and it was obvious that Cletus' statement hadn't even put a hitch in his giddy-up.

"They said they backed off the damn thing, and they thought sure it was the last night they'd spend fishin'—but just then a deer broke through the brush. Something else spooked it, I guess, and this—this THING saw it and turned. Before they could get movin' back toward the bridge, they saw it crush the deer—one bite. One *bite* Cletus...damndest thing..."

"What kind of beer were they drinking, Jaz?" Cletus asked. "And how much? I might believe—probably not, but for argument's sake, let's say I might—that there was a lost gator out there, or even a really big gar with the right shadows. Hell, some idiot might have let loose a double-d-goddam pet anaconda in there...but, just between you and me, there are no dinosaurs in the Perquimans River."

" 'Cause you ain't seen one?" Jasper asked.

Cletus laughed and downed the rest of his beer, waving at Willow for another pitcher.

"Because there are no dinosaurs in *any* river. There are *no dinosaurs* at all. Are you puttin' me on?"

Jasper frowned.

"I'm tellin' you what they said, Cletus. They didn't look like they were joking. Max Nixon looked ready to have a cow, you want the truth. They had beer, sure, but no more than usual, and both those boys know the difference between a damn dinosaur and a gar, or a snake."

"That may be true," Cletus said, "but that doesn't change the fact that there's no dinosaurs in the Perquimans River or in The Great Dismal Swamp, so where in hell did it come from?"

"You really got to ask me that?" Jasper said, eying Cletus with disdain. "We're not that far from a ton of military bases up in Virginia. You've seen *Jurassic Park*, and I guess I don't have to remind you about what can happen when you mix a deer and a man too close…"

Cletus sat back and stared.

"That was different," he said.

"How?" Jasper asked. "I found that guy stickin' boot first out of the swamp, and you believed me then, didn't you?"

"That was you, Jaz," Cletus said, "and I saw it myself. Hell, Bob saw it too."

"Well, I guess we're goin' to have to go and see for ourselves, then," Jasper said. "I got that boat, and we're goin' fishin' anyway. I say we go in a little deeper than we planned. I know where Max said he saw that thing take the deer. Anything the size he's talking about would leave sign, and we've been hunting those swamps since we were boys."

Cletus had a sinking sensation in his gut. Willow showed up then with a new pitcher, and he was so distracted he didn't even thank her as he reached for it and began to pour. Every time. Every damn time he and Jasper set out to go fishing, something crazy happened.

"Maybe we should just stay home and watch the race," he said.

"You know we're not gonna do that, Cletus," Jasper grinned. "Hell, I bought me that .50 caliber BMG at the auction… I can mount that sucker on the boat, just in case."

Cletus stared at his friend in disbelief.

"You *bought* that thing? Have you ever shot it?"

"Well, no," Jasper said. "They won't let me use it over at the range, but I got some ammo, and it came with a tripod. Hell, Cletus, it's just a gun."

"Jaz, it's a freaking cannon," Cletus said. "You shoot that thing it will send the boat a hundred yards back downstream, if it doesn't knock your shoulder loose—or your brain. You do still have one, yes? Are you seriously telling me our fishing trip is turning into a dinosaur hunt?"

Jasper only grinned. "We could take the boat, and *leave* the gun," he said. "Of course, considering our track record, we might as well go up that creek without a paddle, you know?"

Cletus dropped his head to the bar and counted very slowly from one to ten. Willow, who happened to be walking by just then, patted him on top of the head. Jasper poured another beer and glanced around the bar.

"Glad that's settled," he said. "You want to play some pool before we go, Cletus, or you going to just nap on the bar?"

Cletus sat up and grabbed his beer.

"You rack," he said. "I need to get some serious drinking in before tomorrow morning, and I don't want any interruptions."

Jasper clapped him on the shoulder, stood, and grabbed the pitcher. They headed for an open table in the rear of the club. If he fed Jasper enough beer and kept him up late enough, Cletus wondered if his buddy would forget the whole thing. In his gut he knew the answer. He hoped the .50 caliber wouldn't sink the boat, or, if it did, that they'd at least be close to shore and his truck when it happened.

"Why," he asked no one in particular, "can't we just go double-d-goddam fishing?"

7

The doorbell to Cletus' trailer buzzed at 5:30 AM. Cletus, who had secretly been hoping that Jasper had consumed enough beer the previous night to dissuade him from his plans, raised his head and glanced blearily at the door to his bedroom. He waited. The bell rang again. Then, as if Jasper had passed out forehead first on the button, it started ringing and just kept on—a loud, uneven cacophony that threatened to jar what little conscious thought Cletus could muster into oblivion.

With a groan, he rolled off the side of the bed, not bothering to reach for a robe, or a shirt. Jasper had seen him in his boxers before, no reason to think one more time would send him over the edge.

By the time he reached the door, the buzzer was faltering, nearing the end of its useful life. It wasn't meant for sustained sound, and Cletus cursed under his breath.

"Alright, damn it!" he called. "I'm coming, Jaz, let off the damn doorbell before you bust it!"

There was another long moment of sound, and then, with a sort of fizzling jitter, it died. The buzzing continued to echo through Cletus' sleep-fogged mind, but at least the throbbing pain subsided. He found his way to the door, unlatched the chain, and pulled it open.

Jasper stood outside, grinning like an idiot. He was head-to-toe camouflage, from the wading boots to the ball cap. In the driveway Cletus saw Jasper's truck, and behind it on a wobbly rust-spotted trailer, rested the new boat. Just like he'd threatened the night before, Jasper had mounted his new .50 caliber up near the front on a tripod. It looked like something out of a bad remake of *Creature from the Black Lagoon* and Cletus stifled a groan.

"What time is it?" he asked.

"'Bout an hour past fish breakfast," Jasper said. "I told you I'd be here early, Cletus. You just getting' up?"

Cletus glanced down at his boxers, then glared at his friend.

"Is it that obvious? Come on in and make some damned coffee. I'll get dressed."

Jasper followed him inside and headed for the kitchen. It wasn't the first time Cletus had been late rising for a planned outing, and Jasper knew where the coffee, filters, and just about everything else in the place was kept. Cletus left him to it and headed back to his bedroom.

He glanced longingly at the short hall leading to his bathroom. He knew a shower would change his outlook on the day, but he also knew that if he tried to get one in, Jasper would become entirely impossible to deal with.

He fished through the mostly clean flannel shirts and jeans and found some that didn't seem likely to make him itch too much. He checked his wallet and keys, and picked up, in careful order, all of the things he could not do without on a daily basis, dropping them into various pockets and ticking them off in his mind.

For years he'd chronically misplaced things. The number of times he'd turned up at a store without his wallet, forgotten his house keys, or misplaced a cell phone was legendary. The solution he'd worked out over time was a very simple one. Before he went to bed, he emptied his pockets onto a tray on his dresser. Wallet, keys, mp3 player, even the tiny lock pick set he regularly carried. He arranged them carefully, and then, when he rose and dressed, he put each thing in the same pocket—wallet left hip pocket, comb right hip pocket, car keys and mp3 player, right front pocket, house keys and lock picks left front pocket. He hadn't misplaced any of these items in several years. He'd even thought about writing an article about it for some online journal, or maybe for one of the tabloids he reported for on a freelance basis. Part of the reason he hadn't was the thought of explaining why he needed lock picks.

Ten minutes later, teeth brushed, his hair semi-combed and tucked back under an old U. S. Navy ball cap he'd picked up at a thrift store and a deep scowl etched across his features, he emerged into the living room. Jasper was seated on the couch, the TV blaring and tuned to ESPN.

Cletus stalked to the kitchen and grabbed a coffee mug. He didn't want to admit it, but now that he was actually awake and moving, with the scent of freshly brewed coffee filling his lungs, he was almost glad Jasper had shown up. They hadn't been out in a long time, and he knew a lot of that was his own fault. He had too many jobs. Journalist, common-law lawyer, ordained minister, private investigator—he did well for himself, but mostly because he scrambled constantly, moving from one job to another. Sometimes it was hard to find breathing room, and he and Jasper had been fishing, hunting, and running around the swamp since they were boys. They'd seen some things most men wouldn't even believe were possible, and it was about time they had a day just to get out on the river and commune with the catfish.

By the time he turned back toward the TV, he was actually grinning.

"You get the beer?" he asked.

"What do you think?" Jasper grinned. "I had to slip it out past Pap, but I got two twelve packs in the cooler in the back of the boat. I don't reckon we need that much, but it never hurts to be prepared."

"You know how to drive that boat?" Cletus asked. "You get it licensed, got the stickers in place…"

"I do," Jasper said. "Day I bought it, Bob was in the crowd. He came up to me right after, like he didn't trust me or something, and gave me the papers to fill out. Can you believe that guy?"

"He's keeping you out of trouble," Cletus said, his grin widening. Sheriff Bob had been through some of their oddest adventures with them, and he knew Cletus and Jasper better than any lawman ought to. "He knew you'd just take it out and forget, so he set you on the right track."

"Whatever," Jasper said. "Pain in my butt. Had to go over to Eerie Haste's in Hertford and register it. Did you know you have to pay *taxes* on a damn boat?"

"I did," Cletus replied. "It's one of the reasons I don't have one. We've always caught enough fish from the shore, and honestly, it's harder to fall into the river from the bank than it is from a boat."

"Pansy," Jasper said.

"Maybe," Cletus said, "but I've been in that river. There's more snakes in it than fish, and I've seen snappers as big as wash tubs. Now you tell me there's a double-d-goddam dinosaur in there, so you want to chase it in a fifteen-year-old, second-hand bass boat with a freaking half-legal cannon mounted in the bow. Pardon me if my excite-o-meter isn't pegged."

"We got to do it," Jasper said calmly. "If we don't, Max White and his buddies will get back in there, and we'll miss out."

"On what? Either looking like fools, or, less likely, being eaten by a dinosaur?"

"Christ, Cletus, for a journalist you sure can be dense. The *story*! We got to take your camera. If we see that thing, or find tracks, or even a big hole in the brush—like bigger than a mad bear would make—we got a story. You could write it up for *The Weekly Globe*. Heck, if it's good enough, we might get some of those ghostbusters from cable in here."

"They don't chase dinosaurs, Jaz, they chase ghosts."

"Not all of 'em..." Jasper said. "There's one Pap likes where they sit around at the beginning of the show and go over all the stories that have been sent in, then decide which ones to check out. I'm tellin' you, this could be big."

"Whatever," Cletus said. "Just make sure the beer is cold. You can hunt all the dinosaurs you want, I'm counting on fried fish for dinner."

Jasper just grinned. He gulped what was left of his coffee, and Cletus followed suit.

"Let's get out of here," he said, "before I decide the day would be better spent crawling back into bed and forgetting the whole thing."

Jasper backed the trailer into the water at their regular fishing hole, and Cletus was surprised to see that his buddy almost looked like he knew what he was doing. A few moments later they'd cranked the boat loose from the trailer and pulled the truck up around the side of a line of trees near the road.

The cooler, bait, tackle and Cletus' camera bag were stowed in under the seats. Jasper set the choke, turned the key, and after only a couple of sputters, the engine kicked to life and began idling.

"I'll be damned," Cletus said. "We might actually get away from the shore."

They settled in, and Jasper backed the boat out into the main channel, turning north toward the Great Dismal Swamp. They'd both explored the banks of the river, camping out on the banks, and at times on raised platforms in the middle of the water itself, up away from prowling animals. They'd fished the river from canoes, but not recently. The older they'd gotten, it seemed, the more appealing a lawn chair on the bank became.

"We should have gotten one of these a long time ago," Cletus said at last. "This is actually comfortable, not like those hard wood seats in the canoe. Also, I don't have to worry as much about your drunk ass standing up and tipping us into the river. This might work out."

Jasper scowled at him, but he couldn't hold it. His expression shifted to a grin.

"I told you it would be good," he said. "We're going to find some new spots for catfish, and maybe bass, and who knows what else."

They rounded a bend, and off to the left the river opened up a bit. There was a patch of weeds along the bank.

"This looks like a good place to try," Cletus said. "I'm thinking something big might be hiding away in those weeds."

Jasper slowed their progress, but he frowned.

"Already?" he said. "I thought we'd be going on into the swamp."

"The day is young," Cletus said. "I don't know about you and your dinosaurs, but I came out here to catch some fish, and I think that's a good spot. Might even be a bass or two in there..."

Jasper cut the motor, and the boat drifted along slowly. Then, as if he'd been doing it all his life, he loosened a line at the rear of the boat and let the anchor slide to the bottom. It caught with a soft jerk, and the boat held against the gentle current.

Cletus reached for the two rods he'd brought. One was rigged for bottom fishing, a sinker with several inches of line beyond it and a treble hook. The other he planned on using to cast for bass, once the first was out and ready. He always released the bass he caught—the first rod was for catfish, and those would be going home with him. There were few things Cletus liked better than a good deep-fried chunk of catfish.

If he got hold of a gar, he thought he might haul that home too. He and Jasper had brought one in once. It took them half a day and a hacksaw to clean the damn thing, but once they got to the meat, they'd chopped it into chunks and dropped it into Cletus' "Fry Daddy" deep fryer. Against all the odds, the meat had been sweet, and good—more like chicken than fish. He didn't look forward to the initial battle of preparation, but he thought he'd sure like to try eating one again.

All of this was going through his mind as he worked to bait his hook and choose a lure. That probably accounted for his missing the sound of an approaching engine until the other boat was almost on top of them.

"What the hell?" Jasper said.

They turned just in time to see the prow of a big, metal-flake monstrosity of a bass boat roaring down the center channel of the river. Max Nixon was bent over the wheel, and Bill White was holding on for dear life in the back seat.

The boat was headed right for them, and moving fast. Jasper lunged for the controls, but it was too late to do anything. At the last second, Max swerved, sending a sizeable wake broadside against them. Cletus hung on and leaned against the first pitch, already regretting his assumption they were less likely to get dunked than they'd been in a canoe.

The boat rolled, tipped violently back the other way, and then, slowly, settled.

Cletus didn't move until the rocking slowed and then, eventually, stopped. Jasper lay half across the front seat, near the wheel and controls. As the boat stopped moving, he started cursing and clawing his way forward.

"What are you doing?" Cletus asked.

"What the hell do you think?" Jasper asked. "I'm goin' after that jackass."

"Why?"

Jasper turned and glared at Cletus.

"What the hell do you mean *why*? Cletus, the bastard nearly dumped us in the river."

"And what would you do if we caught him?" Cletus asked.

Jasper stared at him. "I…"

"That's what I thought," Cletus said. "Sit down…let's catch us some fish. We can report Max to Bob when we get back, if you're still pissed."

Jasper continued to glare at him, but he made no more moves toward the ignition.

"They got to come back this way anyway," he grumbled. "We'll hear 'em coming this time, and I'll be ready. Ain't no call to be racin' down the river like that. Could have swamped us."

"Hand me a beer, Jaz," Cletus said. "I hear a catfish calling my name, and I think I'm going to listen. If ol' Max didn't scare off all the fish, I'm counting on taking some home."

"Yeah, whatever," Jasper said. He reached into the cooler, grabbed a beer and tossed a second to Cletus. "Just pisses me off, that's all."

"You and me both, brother," Cletus said. "You and me both…"

The day moved slowly from then on, just the way Cletus had hoped it would. They pulled in three or four catfish, one going nearly three pounds, and they'd dropped them into the live-well at the back of the boat. It was kind of nice having the boat, seeing how the other half of the fishing world lived.

Cletus patiently tossed a variety of lures into the weeds near the bank, but with the exception of a single boiling swirl of water that might have been an aborted strike, he had no luck with the bass. It didn't matter. They drank the beer slowly, relaxed in the surprisingly comfortable seats, and pulled in the catfish.

"You got any charcoal?" Jasper asked.

"I keep bags of it out back in the shed," Cletus said. "You know that. I even have a spare grill in case rust and Mother Nature take out the one I've been using. We get back, we'll skin these on the bank, drop 'em in the cooler and have them grilling by sunset. We even have enough beer...go figure."

Jasper seemed content, but Cletus noticed his friend glancing up the river now and then, and he knew the insult of that other boat flashing past hadn't dropped off the radar just yet. The sun was getting pretty high in the sky, and the fish were biting a lot less frequently.

"You about ready to call it a day?" Cletus said. "I think we have enough for a couple of meals."

Jasper didn't look happy.

"I reckon," he said, "but..."

Before he could finish, there was a loud *CRACK!* They both jumped, and Cletus nearly dumped himself in the river catching his balance. The sound repeated, and Jasper dove for the boat's ignition.

"Reel in, Cletus," he said. "That's gunshots."

Cletus was already reeling.

"I know what it is, Jaz, but what..."

"Don't know, but it's coming from up river, and that's where Max and Bill went."

"So? Maybe they found a buck..."

"They ain't hunting, Cletus. Deer season's months away."

Jasper was moving as he spoke. He had the engine started, and Cletus yanked his line, drawing in the lure he'd been using and reeling quickly to keep it from slapping him in the face. He dropped the rod and grabbed the other. He'd barely started reeling when Jasper brought the boat to life and started sliding out over the water.

"Hold on," Cletus said. "You're gonna..."

Just then, his line went taut. He didn't know if it was a fish, a log, or a snag in the weeds, but he was never going to find out. Jasper gunned the engine, and they shot off across the water. Cletus' rod bent, bent some more.

"Jasper!" he yelped.

It was too late. The line parted with a crack like a whip. Whatever had been yanking on the other end of it, stayed where it was, and Cletus toppled over backward into the boat, landing on his ass and smacking himself in the face with the rod.

"Goddamit, Jasper!" he said, tossing the rod to the floor of the boat and turning. "I said to *wait*."

Jasper was paying no attention. He was bent over the wheel, spinning the boat around the bend with surprising control, particularly considering the amount of beer they'd already consumed. The banks were lined with cypress knees and dangling brush, but the central channel, at this point, was clear. Jasper gunned the engine, and the old boat shot across the water. Ahead there was another curve to the right, but Jasper throttled back, caught it just right, and shot around the corner.

Cletus made a mental note to ask when his buddy had learned to drive a boat like that, but decided it was the better part of valor not to interrupt when they were moving at high speed.

Another rifle cracked, and this time they could also hear, barely over the roar of their engine, a voice screaming.

They spun around the corner and Jasper cut the engine so quickly the boat shuddered, and the engine died. They slid forward a few more yards, the prow of the boat plowing into the water and sending out a large wake.

Ahead, nose down in the river, motor dangling in the air, was the other boat. The propeller still spun lazily. There was an old blue plastic cooler floating off toward the far bank, and a ball cap—the one that Bill White had been wearing—floated on the water near the boat. There was no sign of the two men.

"Japser," Cletus said.

His friend paid no attention. The boat floated slowly closer to the other craft, picking up speed in the current.

"Jaz!" Cletus said, voice louder. "JAZ!"

Japser turned.

"Start the engine," Cletus said. "Now!"

Jasper turned, stared stupidly at the controls, then reached down and turned the key. At first all that happened was a wild sputter. Then, on the second turn, the engine gurgled to life.

Something crashed in the brush to the right of the river. Something big.

Jasper stared off into the trees.

"Jasper," Cletus said, lunging forward and yanking on his friend's pants leg. "You either get forward to that gun, or get us the hell out of here…"

That did it.

Jasper started to move then, like he was waking up from some sort of dream. Cletus braced himself for the boat to spin and tear out back down the river, but that didn't happen. Jasper opened the throttle, just slightly, and turned so that they were headed toward the overturned boat.

"What the hell are you doin'?" Cletus said.

Jasper glanced back at him and frowned.

"We have to see what happened, Cletus. What if they're hurt?"

"You picked a fine time to get heroic," Cletus said. He turned and stared up the river, scanning the banks for any sign of movement.

There was another crash, but it seemed farther away. They approached the capsized boat slowly, and Jasper spun the wheel gently so that they came alongside it on the opposite side from the closest bank. He dropped the engine into neutral, letting it idle, and moved toward the front of the boat. As they reached the upended bass boat, he reached out and grabbed it, drawing them alongside.

Cletus stood carefully and glanced into the boat. There was a mess of tackle, food, and beer cans lodged in and around the seats. The water rose half the length of the boat, which appeared to have been jammed nose first into the muck at the bottom of the river.

There was no sign of Max or Bill at first. Then he heard Jasper gasp, and he glanced up and followed the line of his friend's gaze to the bank. In the weeds by the bank, an old ball cap bobbed lazily in the water. Beyond that there were a series of deep ruts gouged into the bank. When he followed those ruts up out of the water, and out of sight, Cletus saw what had gotten Jasper's attention. There was a single stained boot lying in the muck, half buried, as if something large had rolled over the top of it. Protruding from the boot about six inches was what was left of a man's leg.

Suddenly, the river seemed very silent.

"Max?" Jasper called out softly. "Bill?"

There was no answer. Even the birds and insects seemed to have been muted.

"What the hell, Jaz," Cletus said.

"I don't know, Cletus…what do we do?"

Cletus wanted to say, *put 'er in gear and head back down that river until this is nothing but a bad memory*, but he knew it wasn't going to happen. They'd stepped right in it, and it was deep.

"There's no one out here," he said. "I guess we could pull up to the bank and see if we can find any sign of 'em."

Jasper reached down without looking, grabbed his beer, and downed it in a single swallow.

"Hand me another, Cletus," he said. "I'm gonna get us in there so you can step onto that bank, then I'm going to get behind that gun there. If you hear me yell at you, you drop. Whatever you're doing—drop."

Cletus started to ask why *he* had to be the one that got out of the boat, but he knew the answer. Jasper had control of the boat, and had shown considerable skill with it. He also knew how (in theory) to fire the damned .50 caliber mounted on the bow. Cletus had no gun, but he did have a camera.

"Hold on," he said. "Let me get some shots of those ruts and the drag marks. When I get out there I'll snap a couple of that boot, but I ain't touchin' it. We're going to have to get Bob and his boys out here, and I don't want to be accused of muckin' up a crime scene."

"Crime?" Jasper said. "Cletus, it's a damn dinosaur, weren't you listening?"

"Might be a bear," Cletus said. "Might be crazy people too… we've seen enough of those around for a lifetime. Might even *be* a gator, though it would have to be a damned big one. One thing it is *not*—at least until we have a picture of it—is a double-d-goddam dinosaur."

"But…"

"Jaz, shut up and get me in to that bank."

They floated in closer, and Cletus moved to the side of the boat. Jasper let the boat turn into a slide across the last few feet, until it bumped gently against the cypress knees and soft mud.

"You be careful, Cletus," Jasper said. "I don't care if it *is* a bear, you watch your ass."

"Tell you what, Jaz," Cletus said, stepping carefully out of the boat and onto the bank. "I'm gonna watch where I'm going. You can watch my ass if you want…"

The camera Cletus had brought was digital and light. He'd hung it around his neck, and as he moved forward, he thumbed the button that brought it to life. There was a soft ding, and a whirring sound as the lens popped out the front of the camera. Cletus froze, waiting to see if the sound would alert whatever was out there. His heart kept pace with the idling motor of the boat, pounding blood through his ears.

He stopped and took several shots of the strange marks on the bank, and several more of the boot and its gory cargo. He had to fight back the urge to lose perfectly good beer at the sight, but he knew he had to get what he could for Bob. They couldn't be sure animals wouldn't disturb the scene. Hell, they didn't know that whatever *caused* the scene wouldn't come back.

He turned away from the boot and tracked the drag marks that followed on beyond. As he moved farther from the bank, the ground became slightly firmer and drier. He was looking so hard for movement in the bushes, or more signs of a body, that he nearly stepped right into what appeared to be a hole of some sort. He stepped back, and stared. Then he leaned in closer, his eyes growing wide.

Not a hole. Not a divot or a poorly concealed root.

"Christ on a stick," he said softly.

"What is it?" Jasper called softly. "Cletus, where are you?"

Cletus didn't answer. He stepped back, because it was the only way to get the proper perspective for the shot. He started to snap photos then, moving in a slow circle, forgetting the woods, the river, Jasper, and even the dead man's foot two yards behind him in the mud.

It was a track. The biggest double-d-goddam track Cletus had ever seen. Near the front, deep gouged claw marks pierced the earth. The center of the track was an impossibly long stretch of flattened brush and mud, pressed at least half a foot deep, and trailed by a single claw scrap, not as pronounced, like it might almost have come from some sort of dewclaw. Cletus caught every angle he could think of. In a sudden burst of inspiration, he found a branch that had broken off when whatever this thing was had passed. He laid it beside the print so that the base of the branch rested by the back claw mark. He snapped a last photo.

Then a sound rose. It wasn't close, but it was loud—so loud and so deep it stood every hair on his neck, head, and arms on end and shivered down his spine. It was a roar, and a scream—something impossible. His legs went weak, and he nearly dropped, but he got control of himself, snatched up the branch he'd used for perspective, and ran for the bank.

He leaped into the boat, sending it rocking, and Jasper didn't wait for him to speak. The engine roared, and they spun out and away, skimming the bank for just a moment before cutting into the center of the river and away. Neither man looked back.

8

"Let me get this straight, Cletus," Sheriff Bob said, his frown deep and etched solidly across his lean features. "You're tellin' me something down the Perquimans River left that... print. You're tellin' me that Max Nixon and Billy White are gone, except maybe whatever's dangling out of that boot, and you boys—you and Jasper—just happened to be there when it happened."

"There isn't time for this, Bob," Cletus said. "It's going to be dark soon. You'd better get the troopers out there, and I think you'd better call fish and game. We're going to need a search party, and it's not going to be easy to get anyone to join it if they see those tracks."

Bob glowered. It was a bit more impressive than his frown, but Cletus knew both expressions well, and ignored it.

"Damn it, Cletus," Bob said at last. "This better not be some kind of joke. I swear to God, you get me out there and it's all a setup—you make me look like a fool—and it's your ass."

"You know better than that, Bob," Cletus said.

He met the other man's gaze, and Bob deflated like an old balloon.

"I guess I do," he said. "We've seen some things..."

"Nothing like this, Bob. I mean that seriously. Not with those twins, and not with Foreman James. Hell, even when that guy Donovan was through here and things got weird with Nettie again, I didn't see anything like this."

Bob shook his head. He leaned forward, slapped his hand down on the intercom.

"Colleen, get me the State Police, quick now."

He turned back to Cletus.

"You and Jasper are going to have to show us," he said. "If I'm going out there after whatever made that track, you're going to be right there beside me."

Cletus took a deep breath. He didn't want to go back out there. He didn't want to go within a country mile of that place, but he knew Bob was right. The sheriff and his men could find the place easily enough, but it would be faster with a guide, and if anything had changed—if the evidence had shifted—they were going to need Cletus to show them which way the thing had gone.

"I'm in," Cletus said. "Of course, Jasper might not be in any condition to drive the boat…"

"We'll take our boat," Bob said. "Meantime, you might want to tell him to get that damned cannon off the front of his and tuck it away somewhere before I confiscate it. Jesus, Cletus, you can't just drive down Highway Seventeen with a mounted fifty-caliber without drawing attention."

Cletus blinked. Then, without warning, he burst into laughter. He bit it back because he felt it threatening to fly out of control.

"I'll do that," he said. "You might want to confiscate it, though. You might want to have it with you…"

Bob's glare returned, and Cletus rose.

"I'll just wait outside with Jaz," he said.

Bob didn't reply. As Cletus exited the office, he heard his old friend pick up the phone and start talking. He didn't envy the man the job ahead.

"We got some dead fishermen," Bob said. "And some strange evidence. I think we're going to need some support on this. Yeah, out on the river…"

Cletus closed the door behind him, steadied his breathing, and walked past Colleen's desk and out into the parking lot beyond. The afternoon sun was half-obscured by dark, roiling clouds. In the distance, out over the bay, heat lightning flashed, and in the distance the deep rumble of thunder shivered through the air.

"All I wanted," he said to himself, heading for Jasper and the boat, "was some damned catfish…"

The storm was a big one. Between fish and game, and the state troopers, they'd managed to pull in a couple of bigger boats, but the water was rough and rising as they pulled out into the river. Cletus, wrapped in a slicker he'd borrowed from Bob, huddled next to Jasper in the back of one boat, driven by Wylie McMullan, a local game warden who'd volunteered for the trip. Bob and a pair of state boys rode in a second boat, just a bit behind.

"How far in, you think, Cletus?" Wylie called out over the roar of the boat's engine and the steady rhythm of the rain. "Not sure how long we can stay out here in this…"

"Not far," Cletus said.

They'd dropped the boats at the same spot he and Jasper had used earlier that day. Jasper had griped the whole time about how they were giving away their secret spot, but he and Cletus both knew there was no secret. Every kid who'd grown up near Old Mill for the last thirty years knew it, along with a handful of others, and Cletus didn't think the troopers were out here to lay claim to prime catfish holes. Neither of them had smiled since their arrival, and the boat trip in a storm had done nothing to improve their mood.

"We stopped just ahead," Cletus said. "See where the weeds are still poking through? It wasn't so deep then, but we were here when we heard… what we heard."

Wylie glanced over at him and frowned. Cletus and Jasper had been deliberately vague with Wylie, and Bob had kept the story to himself, for the moment, sharing only the pictures of the print, and the boot, with the troopers. Cletus knew that if Max and Bill had been down to the Cotton Gin running their mouths the night before, Wylie would know something was up. Old Mill, Elizabeth City, Hertford, all of them were small communities and while there was a certain amount of transient population due to the Coast Guard base, most folks knew, or knew of one another. A story like a dinosaur in the swamp would have spread like the fire they used to burn off the cotton fields.

They rounded the corner, spotlights illuminating the river ahead, and Cletus saw the hulk of Max's boat still jammed nose first into the river ahead.

"There!" he called. "See it?"

"I'm not blind, Cletus," Wylie said. "Jesus, what in the hell did that? I mean… the damned nose is stuck on the bottom like someone pounded the other end with a big hammer."

Cletus didn't reply immediately, when he did, he laid a hand on Wylie's shoulder.

"Over there is where we found… the boot."

Wylie worked the boat carefully over toward the bank. The rain was really pouring down. Cletus directed him in close where Jasper had sat earlier, and when they were close enough, he stood.

"We can't stay in here too long," Wylie said. "This storm is picking up, and the river won't be passable."

Cletus nodded. "I have to get Bob and those troopers in there… I imagine they'll be carting out what's left. Unless they plan on following whatever did this out into the swamp tonight, I doubt we'll be here long."

The second boat pulled in, it's bow pointed into Wylie's bow, and one of Bob's deputies reached over to take a line and hold them fast. Bob stepped ashore, and Cletus followed suit. Jasper stayed in the boat, and Cletus didn't figure any amount of money would pry him loose. One of the troopers followed Bob, and the three of them headed in away from the bank.

They didn't have to go far. The rain had washed down and soaked it, clearing away the blood, but the boot lay right where Cletus had left it. Bob pulled a plastic bag from his pocket and snapped it open.

"Get that damn thing in here, Cletus," he said.

Cletus stared at him.

"Me? Why do I have to put in there? I don't want to touch that damned thing, Bob"!"

"Somebody get it in there," the trooper said. He was a big man, with a deep scowl, and he was obviously not too happy to be out on the river in the rain. Bob started to argue, and Cletus sighed.

"Just hold that damn bag still," he said. He gripped the boot by its heel, trying not to hold on too tight. It was heavy, though, and in the end he had to use both hands, tip it up, and upend it into the bag. The weight of it nearly tore it free from Bob's grip."

"Christ, Cletus, you didn't have to throw it."

Cletus wasn't listening. He'd already turned and headed back toward the trees. The rain was really coming down, and he was afraid he knew what he was going to find, but he had to get Bob back there, and he had to try.

The others followed close on his heels. He stopped just short of where he knew the track should be, but the ground was dark and running with water. He glanced to the left, then to the right. Bob stopped beside him. The trooper stepped up next to Bob.

"What are we looking for?" he asked. "More body parts?"

"No," Cletus said. "There's…"

The trooper took a step forward and his booted foot dropped down into what seemed to be a hole. He cried out, and Cletus lunged, trying to grab the back of the man's jacket. He was too late.

The trooper pitched forward, arms windmilling, and fell face-first into the mud. He lay there for a moment, and Cletus thought he might have hurt himself. Then the man pushed himself up from the muck and rose, first to one knee, and then all the way up. He turned and stared at Cletus.

"You knew there was a ditch there," he said.

"There is not a ditch there," Cletus said. "That was what I was looking for, though. It's too full of water to see, but I have pictures—Bob's seen them."

The trooper turned to Bob then. He didn't look convinced, or happy.

"Let's get the hell out of here," Bob said. "We'll get a team back here tomorrow to start a search."

"If it isn't a ditch," the trooper said, standing still, and still staring at Cletus as though the fall and his soaked uniform were Cletus' fault, "what is it?"

"A track," Cletus said.

"What? What was it? A truck? Hunter with an ATV?"

"Just a track," Cletus said. Then he glanced at the trees, and stared. He raised his hand and pointed at the trees.

He hadn't noticed it the first time he was there, but there was a spot where two medium-sized trees had been snapped. They bent out, as if something had plowed in between them. Beyond the two trees, just visible through the driving rain, was a black hole. There was no way to tell if there had been trees there at one point or not.

"Whatever it was," Bob said, whistling softly, "I think it went thataway."

Lightning flashed then, and a moment later there was a huge CRACK! as it struck farther back in the swamp.

The three turned without another word and slogged back to the boats, Bob carrying the heavy sack, which bounced off his leg with a wet squish at every step.

"Jesus," he said. "Cletus, next time you plan on calling me with a crazy story—send ahead a memo reminding me not to answer."

Then they were back in the boats and heading back toward the trucks. No one spoke. Bob tried his best not to stare down at the bag at his feet. About halfway back to the truck, he lifted it and handed it off to his deputy.

"Don't let it spill," he said. "You get that prepped and off to the lab in Raleigh as soon as the coroner gets a look. I know Mamie Nixon, and Irma White, too. They're going to want to know where their husbands are… one of them isn't going to like the answer."

The deputy looked queasy, but he took the bag and nodded.

"You think they're both dead?" he asked.

"I don't know," Bob said. "One of them sure is. No way he survived having his leg ripped off—whatever did that—and then being dragged off into the swamp. If this rain keeps up, I don't know if we'll be able to track them."

The deputy glanced down at the bag, then away quickly.

"All the same to you, Sheriff," he said, "I'll pass on that search detail. Don't know what did that—bear, maybe? Whatever it was, it's big and pissed off."

"We'll get a party together," Bob said.

"You'll have support," the trooper said, finally getting over his fit of anger at falling in the mud. "I don't know if your friend over there," he nodded to Cletus in the other boat, "was trying to be funny, but whatever dragged that man off is damn dangerous. Whoever—or whatever—did that," he pointed at the bag at the deputy's feet—"is going to pay."

Bob nodded absently. He was thinking about the spot where the trooper had taken his fall, and about the pictures Cletus had shown him. He was thinking about a foot that was more than a yard long, tipped with huge claws. He was wondering just what the hell they were getting into, and wishing like hell that *he* could get out of that search detail, too.

9

Mac leaned in closer to the monitor directly across the desk from him and placed both hands on the touchscreen, sliding his fingers deftly to either side. The central image expanded until it filled about a third of that screen. To either side, other screens continued to scroll data, some in columns of text, others flipping through images and articles and news bites.

The screen he was fixated on displayed sixteen thumbnail-sized photographs, and one larger that he'd separated from the bunch. It was a patch of moist ground. Embedded in that ground was a very large claw print. Mac saw things like this on a daily basis, and most of them slid in and out of his awareness like water over rocks in a stream. Hoaxes. Anthropological sites. Museums. Cryptozoology pages and groups and mailing lists.

He never fixated on a story for its own sake. The essence of what he did was identifying patterns. The images had come to him in an e-mail from North Carolina, a source that Bullfinch had brought in while on a different case. The reason that the image interested Mac was that, after a very short search of online databases and obscure records, he'd matched the print to multiple sources, and there was very little doubt of what should have made it.

Sarcosuchus or Fasolasuchus, he thought.

He scanned several pages of data, taking it in at a glance and storing it for later use. Twenty-three to thirty feet in length. He flipped through the North Carolina photos and stopped on a pair that showed a branch that had been used for perspective. The print was over three feet long. He did quick mental calculations, scanned a few more pages of data on the remains that had been found of both ancient species, and whistled. It still wasn't exactly clear which creature's print he was looking at, but what was clear was that the thing would have to be at least twenty-five feet long.

The door opened and closed behind him, and a moment later he sensed someone standing at his shoulder.

"What is it, my boy?" Geoffrey Bullfinch asked. "I didn't know you were interested in the animal world."

"Take another look," Mac said, stepping aside. "Check the length of that branch and that print. This came in from one of your contacts, a Cletus Diggs of Old Mill, North Carolina?"

Geoffrey nodded. He studied the print.

"Cletus, among other things," he said, "is a journalist. The periodical he is most often printed in is one that will be familiar to you—*The Weekly Globe*. Among other things, you'll find pictures of giant insects held aloft by farmers and the ongoing adventures of a fellow known only as Rat Boy. I assume this must be more of the same?"

Mac shook his head. He reached out, flipped more images around, brought up two columns of newsprint to the left of the images, and on the right, two other pages of text with highlighted segments. First he pointed to the article on the left.

"These images your friend sent are part of an investigation. Two men were killed on the Perquimans River. Neither has been found, though they did find the lower half of one of their legs, still inside the boot, on the riverbank. The investigation is ongoing. The locals are leaning toward a bear attack, or some crazy swamp man on a killing spree. The state police believe the attack was random—and that the trail leading away from the riverbank indicates some sort of all-terrain vehicle. A storm wiped out most of the evidence at the crime scene. Nothing more has been found."

"I take it that Cletus tells another story?" Geoffrey said.

"He does. He says the two men, Max Nixon and Bill White, had been talking the day before they died about having run across a dinosaur in the swamp. Both of them went in armed. When their boat was found, it wasn't exactly capsized, it was pounded nose first into the bottom of the river, as if it had been stood on end and pressed in by a great weight. Neither the local sheriff's office nor the troopers have an answer for that."

"It still seems pretty weak," Bullfinch said at last.

"It would be," Mac said, except that's not all. That print belongs to one of two giant crocodilian critters that died out about a hundred million or so years ago. My calculations put this one around twenty-five feet long. Ten years ago, there were a couple of obscure mentions on a blog about a Sarcosuchus. The blog was written by a lady who used to work in a genetics lab near the swamp—sexing canaries and providing ready-made slides for biology classes. She mentioned a sample they'd received, said she knew no one was ever going to believe them. Their lab was destroyed by a hurricane, and the samples that they carried out with them didn't make it to another lab in time to preserve them. They had a trace, but not enough to prove what they believed.

"Her post was a call, looking for a man named Eddie Dodd. He signed the label on the sample that came in to the lab. It was labeled 'crocodile.' She was hoping to find him and possibly mount an expedition. There was never an answer to her post, and the blog has not been active in several years."

"And?" Geoffrey asked. He'd detected the quickening of Mac's speech, and knew the younger man was only warming up.

"I did another search," Mac said. "I found Mr. Dodd's contact information. A few months before the blog post, he resigned his position. Up until that moment, he was a collector—gathering biological cell samples for a large biological corporation. Prior to his retirement he was very active. His retirement—I hacked into the company database to see if I could find any information on it—was very sudden. It seems as if he came back from that last trip, handed in his equipment, and just walked away. He never even cashed his final check."

"Odd way for a man to behave," Geoffrey said.

"Unless he was running from something, or afraid someone might come looking for him," Mac said. "One of the stomping grounds of Sarchosuchus and Fasolasuchus was South America."

"There have been no more attacks?" Bullfinch asked.

"Not so far, but that's a big swamp. The Great Dismal stretches a long way from civilization, and there would be plenty of food in there for a creature that size. It could have been there for years… something drew it out of hiding, and if it happened once, I have to think it could happen again."

"That is one strange place," Bullfinch mused aloud. "So many strange things have happened there over the years. It falls on a ley line, you know. Very large one, directly beneath the town of Old Mill, and stretching off into the swamp."

"Come on, Geoffrey," Mac chuckled. "You don't believe in that."

Bullfinch raised an eyebrow.

"If you ever get a spare moment," he said, "do a search on the major ley lines, and then cross-reference it to occult and/or paranormal activity. I believe you'll find one of the patterns you are so fond of.

"There's a book," he said, "one you might enjoy. It's quite a modern piece, but I believe the author has latched onto something important. It's called *American Gods*, and it's written by a man named Gaiman."

"Neil Gaiman?" Mac asked.

Bullfinch nodded. "In that novel he writes about the places where lines of power meet—how they draw old powers. Have you ever wondered why thousands of perfectly intelligent people would stop beside a highway for the opportunity to pay too much for a cold drink, and to see the world's largest chipmunk? Roadside attractions… you might want to search those as well. *American Gods* should be required reading for all O.C.L.T. agents."

Mac shook his head. He didn't look convinced, but at the same time Bullfinch could almost hear the wheels turning in the younger man's mind. He knew that once they parted, the searches he'd suggested would be a priority, and he very much wanted to be around to study the results.

"So, what do we do?" Geoffrey asked.

"I'll give R. C. a call," Mack said. "It's his decision."

Mack donned a headset and flicked his fingers across some controls on the panel before him. A moment later he'd nodded his head, listening intently. He spoke a few quiet words, listened again, and then nodded. "He says you should take Isabella—she just returned last night—and go down there. I'm going to forward him a copy of the files to go through—he's in Bermuda but he'll be available intermittently by phone or e-mail."

Geoffrey chuckled. "I'm sure Ms. Ferrara will be up for this, but even a woman of her talents might find a twenty-three-foot crocodile to be a handful."

"You'll be there to rein her in," Mac said. "You know the contact, and you know the area…"

Bullfinch nodded.

"I do. I find myself drawn back to that place fairly often. It calls to me, it seems."

"I'll see what else I can find," Mac said. "I'm going to try to contact the woman who wrote that blog, and then I'm going to track down our retired adventurer and see what he can tell us about that sample, and how it ended up in North Carolina. He may have thought the sample was from a crocodile, just like he marked it, but his sudden retirement and disappearance seem to say otherwise."

"Dinosaurs," Bullfinch said, shaking his head. "I have chased a great many strange things in my life… I have to say that this one has quite taken me by surprise."

"If it's any consolation," Mac said, grinning, "if you catch it, you could drive it by some of the Baptist churches down south and see what they think."

"Oh, no," Bullfinch said. "That won't do. Then they'd be saying they were right all along, and that there have not been millions of years of evolution. They'd probably proclaim the poor creature to be Leviathan and try to slay it."

"They'll have to get in line behind Isabella for that," Mac said. "I'm betting she's going to love this one."

He turned back to the screens then, and Geoffrey headed back to the door.

Without looking up, Mac called after him.

"I'll get a brief and all the data I can find put together. It will be in your e-mail within the hour."

"Thank you, my boy," Geoffrey said. "I'm not quite used to the instantaneous nature of your world, but I *do* appreciate it. Just think if we could e-mail Ancient Egypt…"

"Give me time," Mac said. "I'm working on that."

Bullfinch turned and stared, just for a moment, then shook his head again and left the room. He wasn't certain if Wendell Macklemore was kidding, or simply speaking his mind. He wasn't certain that he wanted the answer.

10

Geoffrey found Isabella in the gym. She was in the middle of a workout, and he took a seat along one wall, watching in admiration as she spun through a series of movements so quick her limbs blurred. The room was designed for simulated combat. A number of automated obstacles lined the place, and the sequences and difficulty could be programmed or set to react randomly. It was another of Mac's inventions—a way to train for combat without requiring others to bear the brunt of your attacks.

A post rose from an opening in the floor, wooden dowels flipping up and out like arms, and whirled. Isabella caught the uppermost arm, flipped into the air, and came down on the far side, clapping her forearms around another board, halting the whirling motion of the post. Her hand shot out, her palm struck a round target on the center of the pole, and it folded, dropping back into the floor.

Without hesitation she turned and ran. A series of rods protruded from the wall she approached, some thick, some thin, some spaced close and others far apart. She ran up the first two, flipped and grabbed one of the upper rods, spun and tucked so her legs did not strike the next in line, then whipped herself back up and through the gap. She maneuvered through the maze of wooden staves with uncanny grace, landing with a soft thud at the far end, one fist on the ground, half kneeling, ready to pounce.

Geoffrey laughed then. He'd seen just such a stance on a recent trip to the cinema. In the film, it had been a man in an iron suit striking the pose.

Isabella turned then, and smiled at him.

"I've been practicing that," she said. "For my film career. I have studied many of your American graphic novels, and I've found several perfect parts I could play."

"That's the rub isn't it?" Geoffrey said. "With you, it's never play. They frown on hurting your co-stars in those films, and I'm afraid you'd find their version of action a bit tame for your taste."

She tossed her long mane of dirty-blonde hair over one shoulder and winked at him. "Perhaps you are right," she said. "I prefer my monsters real, and I prefer to actually kill them. It's a fault, I'm told. R. C. would like me to exercise more compassion." She shrugged. "I believe we call them monsters for a reason. I do not believe they show compassion, and so I meet them on their own terms."

"A great number of innocent creatures, including some very human creatures, have been labeled as monsters," Geoffrey said. "But I didn't come here to debate the ethics of the hunt. How do you feel about…dinosaurs?"

She stared at him. When she saw that he was not kidding, her face split in a broad smile.

"You must be kidding with me," she said. "Such things do not exist. I have seen them in movies…magnificent…but…"

"I assure you," Geoffrey said, "If Mack is correct, and it's a very rare thing when he is not, we are not going to be dealing with something out of a movie. From the images he showed me, if this beast is indeed running loose, it's something like a very large crocodile, twenty-five feet long, several tons in weight. It would be armored, of course, and unlike the crocodiles you'd be familiar with, this one has longer legs, and can travel quickly on land."

"Where?" Isabella asked, suddenly all business.

"North Carolina," Geoffrey said. "The Great Dismal Swamp."

Isabella frowned.

"I do not like the swamps. The ground is too soft, and it is difficult to move quickly. We will be meeting it in its own territory…"

"I'm afraid it won't answer our invitation, even if we send it," Bullfinch chuckled. "We'll have to go in after it. You and I are the only two available…"

"I'm in," she said. "This place is wonderful—the gym, the accommodations—but it is not what I am meant for. I am meant for action, and for the hunt. Without that, I grow restless. I have not slept in two days."

Bullfinch studied her. He decided that she wasn't kidding.

"That is not healthy," he said.

"I am aware," she replied. "There is little I can do. I will not use drugs because I never know when I will need to fight. I work out until I am exhausted, but the result is that I lie in bed, aching and sore and wishing that I was up and moving, hunting. It's in my blood. I will hunt your dinosaur. I *need* to hunt it."

"This won't be any kind of hand-to-hand," Geoffrey said. "We're going to need some serious armament for this job."

"You will leave that to me," Isabella said. Then she actually smiled. "I know a thing or two about weapons, you see, and this will not be my first hunt. I will not even know, until we have faced off with your crocodile, if it is the most dangerous thing I have faced. I will let you know—once it is dead."

"We aren't necessarily going in to kill," Geoffrey said. "If such a thing exists, and we can subdue it, it would be wonderful for science."

"I have seen another of your movies," Isabella said. "In that movie, you took giant, magnificent creatures such as the one you describe and turned them into a sideshow attraction. They reacted as I would react—I respect that. I do not believe your creature will want to be captured."

"You may be right," Geoffrey said. "I believe, in the end, that no matter which of us learns more about this creature… you will be the one to understand it."

Isabella nodded, but did not answer. He could see that her mind had already slid ahead to weapons and planning. In her mind, she was already in the swamp, trying to catch the creature's trail. He hoped, for her sake, that the purpose granted her rest. He'd been in the depths of that swamp, and he'd seen things even he was at a loss to explain.

He turned, then, and left the gym. Isabella was already heading the opposite direction, toward the showers. Geoffrey wanted to get back to the computer console in his room. He knew the data Mac had gathered would be waiting for him, and he also thought he'd better get a note off to Old Mill. Cletus would need to know that they were coming. It wasn't likely the local law enforcement officials would greet them with open arms, even when they presented their credentials. They didn't want to draw any more attention than absolutely necessary.

He also hoped they'd learn something about how this creature was possible—where it had come from, and how. Geoffrey had lived a very long, very odd life. He'd seen, time and again, how circumstances that should have proven impossible—or at the very least, unlikely—occurred with alarming regularity. A number of events had to have transpired to cause this situation, and though he was a man of science, more or less, he was not fully convinced that the things he'd seen, and faced, could be chalked up to coincidence or circumstance. All too often, it seemed something was aligning events to suit a twisted, arcane plan. Just as often, he found himself drawn into the pattern.

"The tangled webs," he said softly. "We weave them to be so complex…"

In his room, Geoffrey pulled out a bottle of red wine he'd been saving, a favorite vintage from the Rioja province of Spain, and uncorked it. He sat the bottle on his desk, with a flat-bottomed tumbler, and logged on to his terminal.

He was perfectly fine with Mac controlling their computer system and their access. It served to protect them all—from within, and from without—and he knew that if he put private information on the network, it would remain private, so long as it wasn't a danger to the team, or to human life. Mac was frighteningly talented with computers, but he was also possibly the most absolutely moral human being Geoffrey had ever encountered.

Before he moved on to the files from Mac, he opened his e-mail program and sent a quick note off to Old Mill.

"Cletus, heard about your… reptilian problem. Doesn't look like

the local law is going to be much help. Will be in town in a few days. Bringing a friend—she's a hunter, but like no hunter you've ever met. Hope you are keeping safe..."

He signed it and sent it. He didn't want to put too much information in the note. Cletus J. Diggs was a man of many talents, and one of them was research. He hoped that he and Isabella would be in Old Mill before the man had a chance to do any real checking up. Not that Mac would allow anything important to be leaked, but it was best to come in clean in a situation like this.

If they could get Diggs to show them the last known location of the creature, they might be able to track it and put an end to the danger before anyone else got involved. If not, if there were other deaths, or they ran into problems, things could get very complicated very quickly. O.C.L.T. operatives worked with the sanction of several governments, but none of it was official, and while wheels could be greased behind the scenes, open confrontation with agents of other agencies, or branches of the law, could be tricky at best.

He poured a glass of the wine, opened the folder Mac had linked him to, and sat back to read.

11

Cletus sat and stared at his monitor. He remembered Bullfinch, vaguely. A man named Donovan DeChance had come through a year or so back. There had been a series of murders, and some very strange occurrences. Then, when DeChance and his friends left, the strangeness had stopped. For a while. It never stayed any form of "normal" in Old Mill.

Bullfinch was an expert in folklore, mythology, things like that. Cletus couldn't figure what the guy thought he was going to do about a double-d-goddamned dinosaur, but he thought it might be nice, for a change, to have someone around who was planning on helping, instead of getting in the way.

Jasper had been back and forth, half the time wanting to mount an expedition into the swamp with a bazooka and a video camera, and the other half wanting to move to another state and forget the Dismal Swamp even existed.

Cletus couldn't blame him. It was crazy. They knew what they'd seen, and what they'd heard. They had the photographs Cletus had taken, and they'd questioned every Tom, Dick, and Harry who might have heard the story Max Nixon told the night before he died. He didn't want go within a country mile of the swamp, but he lived near it. He had fished and hunted there all his life. He had seen things in there that made a dinosaur seem almost common-place, and he'd be damned if he was going to be run off by a giant by-god alligator, or crocodile, or whatever the hell it was.

He typed a quick return message.

"Looking forward to seeing you. Strange happenings in these parts, but I hear you're no stranger to such things. I'll get rooms for you at the bed and breakfast in Old Mill where Donovan stayed. Call when you are close.—Cletus"

He hit *Send* and sat back. He wasn't sure what Bullfinch thought he could do to help, but he *was* sure that he'd run through all the things he himself might do, and didn't like any of them. They still had Jaz's .50 caliber and the boat. If no one believed them, then no one would follow them in. The thing was, there had been no more reports of attacks. There was no sign of the creature at all. It was like it had slipped from the shadows, killed, and then disappeared like one hell of a big puff of smoke.

The worst of it was, Bob knew something was wrong, but he wouldn't pursue it. He'd gone along with the troopers when they said it was a bear, or some wild man in the swamp. He'd told the local news they had it all under control, and he'd assured people things were just fine. Whoever, or whatever, had killed Max Nixon (it had been Max's left boot they'd found—the coroner had managed to get it verified by Max's widow—she recognized his boot, and he had a tattoo of a rooster with a noose around its neck on his ankle so he could tell folks he had a cock hanging below his knee) had taken off for parts unknown. No sign of Bill White had been found at all, and there were even folks saying maybe he'd killed Max and just lit out to avoid arrest.

Cletus didn't really care about the lies. It was fine with him if the news told their version of the truth. He'd written *his* own version enough times for *The Weekly Globe*. What bothered him was that Bob, and the state troopers, were ignoring the danger. They were choosing to pretend Cletus had not taken any photographs of giant tracks in the swamp, and that if something had busted through the trees and off into the swamp, it had been an ATV or a really big bear, nothing more. Men and boys, being what they were, were going to forget soon. They were going to start fishing again. They were going out to their blinds and hunt. They were going to wander along the river, and go canoeing, and soon—maybe not right away, but not that far in the future—someone else was going to die. It pissed Cletus off because he *knew* and he knew that Bob, at least, also knew, and wasn't going to do a damned thing about it.

Just like always, when things in Old Mill got crazy, it was up to him to try and do something about it. He briefly considered grabbing a bottle of whiskey and heading out to see if he could find Nettie. He nixed that idea when he realized that her shack was close to the fishing hole, and that meant it was close to the creature. He didn't believe she was in any danger, but he didn't want to be caught by that thing, sitting around on her porch and drinking cheap whiskey.

It felt different somehow. When he'd gone to her, things had been darker. There had been elements of the supernatural involved, and some damned disturbing memories of his childhood. None of that seemed to relate to the type of danger they faced. If there was a dinosaur in the swamp, Nettie would be as likely to protect it as help kill it. It was her home—her place. If it was there, she knew it was there, and he thought the best he could hope for was that she wouldn't choose sides with him ending up on the wrong one.

He ran through the inventory of his own arsenal in his mind. It wasn't impressive. He had a .45 and an old police .38. He had a 30/30 and a Marlin shotgun, but he didn't think any of them was going to be much use against a dinosaur. The only thing he had that might be of use was a replica black powder .50-caliber buffalo gun. He'd bought it down at an auction in Elizabeth City a few years back, but had never learned to shoot it. He thought maybe, just maybe, it was time he got some instruction.

He wondered if he could track down something a little more modern, and thought maybe he should give Jasper a call. They'd started this together, and just like always, he knew they would finish the same way. Jasper knew people, and he could find the weapons. Cletus thought maybe a bazooka and a couple of grenades were in order. At the very least a few sticks of dynamite.

"Christ on a stick," he said softly. "Why in the *hell* don't I learn not to try and go fishin' with Jasper?"

There was no answer, and with a heavy sigh he stood up and headed for the door. There were things to get done before Bullfinch arrived, and he figured he'd better get started. The sooner they got it over with, the sooner he'd be able to sleep at night. He was pretty sure his double-wide wasn't going to stand up to any dinosaur attacks, so he was going to have to take the fight to that thing.

Maybe, he thought, *I'll even survive to celebrate.*

12

Near the back end of Lake Drummond, the Dismal Swamp gets thicker. There are fewer trails and fewer visitors. There are scheduled hunts in the preserve, and boating and fishing are available on the lake year 'round, but there are depths of wilderness farther in that are all but impassable. During scheduled hunts, there are portions of the preserve closed off to prevent injuries, and things are kept well in hand by park rangers and game wardens.

North Carolina and Virginia, however, are home to a number of different types of hunters and fishermen. Many of these are less than impressed by organized hunts and not inclined to part with the money required for a proper license. Their skills include diversion and stealth. Along with hunting, they pride themselves on their ability to avoid detection, and to hunt when they feel like it, not when someone tells them it's legal.

Ned Peterson and John Tyler Galt were such men. They lived at the end of a seldom-traveled road close on the North Carolina side of the border. There were times, in the winter, or during heavy storms, when their road was impassable. Their shack, built on a platform raised above the ground on the stumps of half-a-dozen felled trees, would have been right at home in a movie about a zombie apocalypse. Their power was supplied by a generator. Their water came from a well they'd drilled themselves. They owned a pickup truck that, when on the road, looked like it had risen from a junkyard of its own volition and might have to be shot in the head to be killed. They had a boat that was painted black and dark green camouflage, draped with cargo nets and nearly invisible when on the lake, or the river, at night. They owned every type of bow, crossbow, rifle and shotgun they could get their hands on, and they kept to themselves.

That was the central focus of their lives—solitude. If no one knew they were there, no one would know when they broke the law. If someone found that a law had been broken, they were not suspects, because they were barely on the radar. There were those who knew them—others they'd grown up with—store owners, gun dealers. They kept their interactions as short and secretive as possible. They paid their bills in cash, and they answered no questions. When they drank, they did so in private.

Still, word travels in small communities. Stories flicker from tongue to tongue and find their way into the deepest shadows. Word of Bill White's disappearance and Max Nixon's death reached Ned and John via the bait shop in Hertford, casually mentioned during an exchange of cash for beer and minnows. The two normally netted their own, but they'd had a slow week, and they needed to get out and set their trot lines. Winter was only a few months away, and they spent much of their summer and fall salting and smoking fish, deer, and bear meat to tide them over. Winters had been hard the past few years, and they didn't want to be caught unprepared.

They listened as the story was related to another fisherman by the old man behind the counter. They didn't meet the man's eyes, and they didn't acknowledge that they'd heard, but they took it all in, and once they had their beer and their bait and were back on the road to home, they worked it over in their careful, no-nonsense way.

Neither of them had ever seen an alligator or crocodile in the swamp, and they'd been as deep in those marshy waters as any two living men. They'd seen some damned big snakes, some strange lizards, and gar that were big enough to be mistaken for logs, but despite rumors of everything from escaped pet anacondas to sea monsters, they'd met nothing in the swamp that didn't belong there. That's not to say the marshes weren't dangerous, just that they were predictable.

After talking for about an hour, remembering everything they knew about the two men who'd had the encounter, and logging onto their satellite Internet feed to do a quick search for reports... they decided that Sheriff Bob was probably right. Nothing stranger than a bear was likely to have attacked the two men, and while it was possible a bear might kill two men, it was equally possible that it had attacked and eaten only one, and that the other had fled into the swamp, gotten lost, and was tucked up in a peat bog dead as a doornail, his bones being cleaned by a variety of vermin and reptiles.

The interesting thing was, there was a reward for the body of the dead man, and the location of, or body of, the second. If a bear had taken them, there would be remains. If one had died and one had run, there would still be remains. In any case, tracking them from the point of the attack shouldn't be that difficult for men used to the swamp. Even if the less-likely scenario was true, and there was a crazy man out there with some sort of ATV and a chainsaw, Ned and John Tyler liked their odds. The reward was $10,000, and that would go a long way toward ensuring a comfortable winter.

"We gotta go in and set the trot lines anyway," Ned said. "Might as well spin in through the river and see what we can find."

John Tyler nodded. "Might as well."

Ned drove in silence for a moment. Then he turned to John Tyler and added, "I'm gonna e-mail Cletus. We get in trouble, he'll have to stand for us."

John Tyler hesitated, then nodded. "Don't tell him when," he said. "We don't need anyone tryin' to follow."

Ned nodded and drove on in silence. Cletus Diggs was one of the best common-law lawyers the state had ever seen, and he knew his way around the Perquimans courthouse. In the past, he'd stood for the two on several cases of poaching, and one case of an unregistered firearm. There weren't many folks in the county who'd stood across the bench from the law who weren't familiar with Cletus. It didn't hurt that he already knew about the missing men—he'd know they were after the reward. Couldn't hurt to have an insurance policy.

The two turned off of Highway 17 and wound off toward the swamp, slipping onto the barely visible dirt road that led to their home. The sun was rising toward noon, and they had a lot of preparations to make.

13

The "Colorado Star" jet landed at a small private field outside Raleigh just after midnight. Bullfinch climbed down to the tarmac and watched as a crew rolled out from the single hangar in the distance to unload their supplies and equipment. Isabella had been very quick, and very thorough. They'd brought their own vehicle, a modified Jeep with a hitch and trailer towing a sleek, dark boat with raised seats. At Bullfinch's insistence, there was no sign of anything official about the vehicles. What the two appeared to be, at least at first glance, was an oddly paired fishing team.

The boat had a powerful outboard engine. It was fitted for fishing, or for a deep hunting expedition. The dark surface of the boat had small flecks of gold embedded in the paint. Across the rear of the craft, carefully scripted in embellished gold-leaf paint, was the word "Raven."

"I wonder whose idea that was?" Bullfinch said.

Isabella, who had been carefully monitoring the transfer of equipment from the jet's ample cargo hold to the Jeep, turned and grinned.

"I think Rebecca named it after you got back from your last adventure. This is not your first trip to the swamp, I am told."

"No, I've been there many times, though only once recently. And yes, it's appropriate. If we have any extra time while we're here, I'll tell you about it and show you some things that are fairly remarkable, even for one such as myself."

"I will look forward to that," Isabella said. She smiled, but he saw in her expression that, as interested as she might be in what he might tell her, she was eager to get out in the field and begin the hunt. He thought back to a conversation he'd had with R. C. Hayes, their de-facto leader.

"She's a wild card, Geoffrey," Hayes had told him. "She has a good heart, but something has sucker-punched it too many times. You have to watch her because once she gets it into her mind that it's time to kill, she can be a little hard to turn off."

Geoffrey hoped that, if it came down to it, he was capable of exerting such control. He'd seen Isabella in action, and he wasn't at all sure there was a man on the planet who could stand up to her if she was angry, or focused.

"If we get on the road tonight," he said, "we should be able to get to the bed and breakfast before morning. That will give us time to get a little rest, and to contact Mr. Diggs."

Isabella nodded. "I will drive first," she said. "You can rest in the Jeep, and then, when we get closer to Old Mill, you will know the way better than I."

"Sounds like a plan," Geoffrey said. "Right now I'm going to go and see if I can find some coffee for the road. You want some?"

"Strong, and black," she said.

Geoffrey smiled, turned, and left her to oversee the rest of the unloading. She doubted the men were going to forget anything, but he knew she would not be satisfied until every detail was to her satisfaction, and that was fine with him. He wanted to stretch his legs, and he really *did* want that coffee.

Geoffrey took over the driving in Greenville, North Carolina. He took it slow, at first, getting the feel of the large vehicle, with its full load and trailer. The roads were quiet, and Isabella wasn't in a talkative mood, so he spent the time going over what he knew and trying to find a pattern to it.

The stories out of Old Mill had to be taken with the proverbial grain of salt. He believed what Cletus Diggs had seen, but that wasn't much. A single track, and a dismembered body. The other two—those who had disappeared after claiming to have seen a dinosaur—he would have discounted entirely, if they had not returned to the swamp and been killed.

The telling evidence, however, had come from Mack. There were enough bits and pieces of a puzzle to get a vague glimpse of the overall picture. The question no longer seemed to be whether there was some sort of dangerous creature in the swamp, but why it had come so close to civilization, after remaining hidden for so long—and when, or whether, it would do so again.

Something large enough to leave the print Cletus had photographed would be difficult to hide in most places, but the Dismal Swamp had deep, dark pits where men simply hadn't traveled. There was ample game in such an environment to sustain a large predator. But something had changed.

Either the creature was outgrowing its environment, or something was affecting that environment, driving it farther from the depths of the swamp in search of food, or to avoid—what?

He knew that Mack was working on just that question. There were myriad interactions between the outside world, and the swamp. For the most part, they were static influences. A great deal of the area was a protected refuge. Other portions were so difficult to reach, with so little to offer, that there was not much likelihood anyone would have a reason to try and reach them.

Still, it is the nature of men to try and explore, change, and in any way possible possess things. The swamp stretched toward cities that were growing steadily—Chesapeake and Suffolk in Virginia, and Elizabeth City spreading out slowly from the North Carolina side. There were new solar power plants cropping up, windmill farms, and always, always the march of paved roads, homes, and industry.

It could be something as simple as chemicals leaking into a waterway—or disease spreading to the creature's food source. Something had shifted, and though it seemed, so far, to have been an isolated incidence, it was possible that the situation that caused it had not changed, and the thing would kill again.

He glanced over at Isabella, who was either dozing or deep in thought, staring out the window into the passing fields. He knew she was confident in her abilities, but he knew, also, that if Mack's information was correct, what they were facing would be well beyond even her experience. The creature in question could grow to a length of nearly thirty feet, and the jaws had already proven capable of cutting a man in two. That wasn't the thing that had disturbed Geoffrey the most.

It was the boat. Something had either picked that boat up and slammed it nose first into the bottom of the river, or had come down on the front with such force and weight that it was pounded in deep enough that river's current couldn't budge it. Something about that took the images in his mind out of any perspective that made sense.

He followed the twists and turns of Highway 17 on past Edenton and Hertford and took the turn-off for the "The Boar and Anchor," a bed and breakfast that had begun its life as a cotton plantation. It butted up against the city of Old Mill, separated by the Queen Street Cemetery. He remembered Donovan DeChance's stories of the place, and the adventures that had led through the swamps and into the lair of a very old, very powerful evil.

He felt a shiver as he drew to a halt in front of the old mansion, and wondered if it was a premonition, or a tingle of power from the massive ley line that bisected the city and the swamp. Or both.

Isabella turned toward him then, and he saw that she was wide awake.

"If you could get us settled," he said, "I'll see if I can get in touch with Cletus Diggs. We should start as early in the morning as possible."

Isabella's eyes flashed, and he thought for just a moment that she was going to insist on heading into the swamp immediately. Then, she turned toward the Jeep and their supplies without a word. Geoffrey pulled out his cell phone and dialed, walking off into the moonlit yard. He didn't believe his companion was going to get much sleep, despite the late hour, but he intended to grab as much rest as possible. If he was going to hunt a dinosaur, or run from one, he wanted his wits about him.

14

Cletus gulped his coffee and stared at the monitor. As e-mail days went, this one was a hum-freaking-dinger. In among the offers to partner with European and Nigerian royalty on money-laundering, ads for male-enhancement drugs and diet aids, he found two keepers.

The first was from Ned Peterson. It was short and to the point.

Cletus,

Me and JT are going into the swamp to set trot lines. Thought we'd take a look see for those two idiots that disappeared. Wanted someone to know we were there, in case something crazy happens—or so you could tell Bob to ask questions first, then shoot, if he's going in too.

See you at the Gin,

Ned

"Damn it," Cletus cursed softly. Ned and John Tyler were probably the two he'd most want beside him if he had to go chasing a dinosaur, but they didn't know. They'd heard some rumor and thought they'd cash in on the reward. They hadn't seen what Cletus had seen, and likely wouldn't, considering the size of the storm that had blown through.

Cletus,

*Isabella and I are in town at the B&B. Will be ready to
set out at dawn.*

Geoffrey Bullfinch

Cletus had never met Isabella, but he'd heard stories. Tall, Italian, beautiful, and a *hunter.* He knew from his experiences with Bullfinch and his associates that it was unlikely they meant hunter in the same sense as Ned and JT would use the term. He wondered if she had any real experience with dinosaurs.

It was just past 6:30. He always woke early, had coffee, checked his e-mail and *then* decided whether to climb back into bed. Didn't seem likely to happen, so he gulped the rest of the first cup and headed to his bedroom to get dressed. On the way he dialed Jasper's number.

It rang several times, then he heard his friend's sleep-clouded voice on the line.

"What?"

"Get up," Cletus said. "Get ready. We have to go into the swamp, and we have to go now. We have us some serious backup, but they aren't going to wait."

"What time is it?"

"Maybe you'd better just not look at the clock," Cletus said. "Might cause less mental anguish. Just get your ass up and ready. I'll be by in twenty minutes."

He hung up and reached for his jeans. It was going to be a hell of a morning.

Jasper was waiting when Cletus pulled up, sitting on a cooler and scowling. Cletus hopped out and helped lift the cooler into the bed of the truck.

"Jesus, Jaz," he said, "what's in this thing? Rocks?"

"Beer," Jasper said. "You said there were two others, and I wanted to make sure there was enough to go around."

Cletus turned and stared.

"We aren't goin' fishin', Jaz. The thing that's in there broke a *boat* and ripped a man out of his boot—minus the foot. I doubt Bullfinch or Isabella are going to be eager to get their buzz on before we go in, or that they'll appreciate it much if you do."

"Tell you what," Jasper said, climbing into the passenger seat and folding his arms. "You *pay* me for this—I figure I'm worth a hundred dollars a day– and I'll leave the beer behind. Otherwise, I ain't huntin' no double-d-goddam dinosaur without beer."

Cletus climbed in and pulled away from the curb.

"Guess you'll be drinkin'," he said. "No one has offered to pay me either. We need to get on over to the bed and breakfast before those two head into the swamp on their own. I doubt they'll get lost, but without a guide, they aren't going to find that fishing hole."

"Who's this Bullfinch clown anyway?" Jasper said. "I never heard a name like that outside a library. And 'Isabella'? Who in hell is *that*?"

"You remember me telling you about that guy DeChance and his buddy Bullfinch. I'm not getting into that whole story again, but Geoffrey's all right. He can handle himself, weird handle or not. Isabella I don't know, but Bullfinch says she's a hunter, and he says it in a way that makes me think she isn't someone you'd want hunting *you*."

"Hell," Jasper said, "if he wants a hunter, he's got us."

"When was the last time you bagged a dinosaur, Jaz?"

"And she has?"

"Don't know, and don't care. I'm thinking any help they can give us is going to be welcome."

"Hope she ain't ugly," Jasper said. He glanced over his shoulder at the cooler longingly.

Cletus gunned the engine and the old pickup shot down the dirt road toward Highway 17. The sun was rising bright and warm to a cloudless sky. At least they'd be able to see where the hell they were going this time.

As they pulled up to the bed and breakfast, Jasper let out an appreciative whistle. Cletus wasn't sure if it was directed at the sleek black bass boat, or the woman standing next to it. Either was worthy.

Bullfinch was sitting in the driver's seat of the Jeep hitched to the boat's trailer. He was bent over a tablet of some type, reading intently. He didn't even glance up, though the woman turned and regarded them coolly. She was as tall as Cletus, maybe taller, slender and athletic with long, dirty-blonde hair and an expressionless, measuring stare.

Cletus started to approach her and introduce himself, thought better, and stepped over to the Jeep.

"You about ready, Geoffrey?" he said.

Bullfinch glanced up, saw Cletus, smiled, and nodded. He turned back to the tablet, read for a second longer, and then closed whatever program he'd been studying.

"Ready as we're likely to be, all things considered," he said. "I just got a little more information on your swamp creature. Mack has been busy. He's been tracking a man named Dodd... I think you can safely rule out bears and crazy fishermen. What we have out there is probably a Fasolasuchus ... should have died out – oh–100 million years ago, give or take. Mr. Dodd found one hanging around in South America—not sure the story on that, but Mack is on his way to see what he can learn. Then he'll be visiting a couple of geneticists who used to live in these parts. By the time we figure out where the thing is—we may have a better idea where it came from."

"Does it matter?" Isabella said, stepping closer. "It has killed, and it will kill again. Wherever it came from—whatever it is—we have to take it down."

"It might be possible to tranquilize…"

"And then what?" Isabella snapped. "Tie it up and put it in a harness? Fly it out with a helicopter and put it on display?"

"I…" Bullfinch fell silent.

"We might not be able to take it down," Isabella said, "but that *is* the mission. You want to study what's left, knock yourself out. This isn't a research expedition—it's a hunt."

She turned then and walked back to the boat, making a pretense of checking their gear for the hundredth time. Bullfinch met

Cletus' gaze and shook his head slightly. Jasper walked back to the pickup, pulled his cooler out of the back, and hauled it over to the black boat.

"What is that?" Isabella asked him.

"Courage," he said. "I'm with you—we kill the damn thing, whatever the hell it is, but I'm not going in there unprepared."

"You have weapons? You have something to give you strength?"

"I got beer, lady. I got a shotgun, and I got beer. You want to go back for *my* boat, I got a fifty-cal mounted and ready for action. Either way—the beer ain't optional."

She watched him struggle to lift the heavy cooler up over the side of the trailered boat for a second, then she stepped closer, grabbed one handle and easily lifted it inside.

"I wish we had your fifty-caliber," she said, "but I'll settle for a shotgun and beer, just as long as it doesn't make you aim it at me, and you know how to shoot."

"I can shoot," Jasper said. "Shot more drunk than sober, so the beer is probably what you'd call an asset."

Cletus climbed into the Jeep behind Bullfinch. Jasper grabbed his shotgun from behind the seat in Cletus' truck, and climbed in the other side. Isabella swung up into the passenger's seat, all in silence. Then Bullfinch turned and glanced over his shoulder.

"If you'll be so kind as to direct us, Mr. Diggs," he said, "I believe we've got a dinosaur to hunt…"

15

The last hook on the trot line had been baited, and Ned leaned back to light a smoke. It was early—they'd gotten in and gotten to work, like always. He and John Tyler had a system, and it worked for them. Neither of them had much patience for sloth or wasted time. When Ned had been a boy, his father had only read him a single bedtime story, and it had stuck with him.

That story was *The Grasshopper and the Ants*. His father had added his own afterword.

"Don't be a grasshopper boy. There's always bad times ahead… but they won't be *as* bad if you're ready for 'em."

Not many waking moments were wasted between Ned and John Tyler, who had a literary legacy all his own. His mother had named him after a character in a book by a woman named Ayn Rand. JT hadn't really understood the stories his mother had told him, but he'd understood his father's simplification.

"It's all about you, boy," the old man had told him. "You do what you can do, and you don't do it for free. You don't give anything away. That book—your ma's never gonna let it go. I never seen so many people ask the same question. Who is John Galt? You be the answer, boy. Don't take nothin' off nobody."

His father had died young, victim of a "drunker" driver in a head-on collision. His mom had followed just a few years back— lung cancer. Too many cigarettes, too many bottles of wine. She'd read all those books but JT had said, only once, that he thought maybe she'd missed the point. His father had worked hard all his life. His mother hadn't done a damn thing for herself, and, after a dozen or more years of his working and her taking advantage of it, JT had moved on. He thought maybe Ayn Rand would understand.

This morning, they'd taken about twenty pounds of catfish for their trouble. The fish were gutted, skinned and iced in the large cooler at the back of the boat. They'd be good all day that way, now they had time to do some hunting.

They knew the place Jasper called "the fishin' hole" well. When they'd been much younger, they'd fished it themselves. Ned killed the motor and let their boat slide past that opening in the trees. There was no one in sight, and he didn't figure there would be for at least half an hour. The type of fishermen who thought this was the place to go weren't too serious, and they weren't likely to be up and about their business before dawn.

"How far down you reckon they went?" JT asked.

Ned scanned the bank to either side and frowned.

"Not too far. Way I heard it, Cletus and Jasper anchored at that first reed bed. That would put the first boat two turns upstream— three at most."

JT nodded. A water moccasin slid out of one of the cypress trees along the bank and wound its way into the river. A bass rippled the water back in the reeds. Other than that, it was so silent they might have floated back in time.

Ned steered away from the reeds and around the first curl in the river. There was nothing ahead except for more water, but the two scanned the shoreline carefully. The storm had washed branches and mud up against the bank. The water was murky and sluggish, and the air was heavy with humidity.

They curled around the tip of an outcropping of roots and entered a straighter section. To their right, the bank was clear. There was no sign anyone had been there recently. Ned started to steer past it, then grunted. He flatted his paddle against the water and brought the boat to a stop in the center of the river.

JT turned and glanced at him, raising an eyebrow. Ned didn't speak; he lifted the paddle from the water again, and pointed the tip of it almost straight down. JT followed the length of it with his gaze and stared into the murky depths.

"Damn," he said. He knelt in the boat and stuck his hand down into the water. He gripped something, and the boat came to a halt. JT pulled harder. At first nothing happened, and then, with a sucking sound, something large let go of the murky bottom. JT held on as the thing shifted. The boat lurched and tipped, but remained upright, and slowly, like a great crocodile rising from the depths, the broken bow of a boat surfaced. It was clotted with weeds and mud, but he'd dragged it free of whatever it had been hooked on.

"Hang on," Ned said. He used his paddle to turn their boat so that it was side by side with the broken hulk. "Let's see if we can drag it up on shore. Might be enough evidence for part of the reward."

"They already seen the boat," JT said. He held on just the same. Ned paddled closer to the bank, and when they were within wading distance, JT hopped out. He stood on the muddy ground, holding the prow of the ruined boat while Ned beached their own craft. He pulled it up far enough to avoid any shift in tide, and tied it off to a gnarled cypress.

The two of them dragged the broken hull of the ruined bass boat onto the bank. Ned tipped it over, so it sat, basically, upright. They stared. It had snapped in half. No way to know what had happened to the rear of the thing. If the stories they'd heard were right, this part had been jammed into the bottom of the river.

"Storm must've busted it loose," JT said.

Ned nodded. He walked slowly around the broken boat, studying the wood. He leaned close and ran his hands over it…then he stopped.

"Holy shit," he said.

JT didn't ask what, he just walked around to follow his friend's gaze. The side of the boat had been punctured by something, like a trident or a pitchfork. There were circular holes gouged through the wood in an arc. Long, deep scrapes ran off from the side farthest from the bow.

JT leaned in even closer and ran a finger into the holes, one by one. He grew very still as he slid his finger into the fourth hole. Without a word, he put his free hand on the other side and pressed.

A moment later he stood, holding what appeared to be some sort of talon or claw. It was only the broken tip—but even the tip was a good two inches long.

"What in the *hell* is that?" Ned asked.

JT frowned and shook his head.

"No idea."

Just then, about half a mile into the swamp, a flock of birds shot into the air, spooked. The air was filled with the sound of flapping wings, and then, suddenly, the river, and the swamp, were very, very quiet.

"What was that?" Bullfinch asked. He stared out over the swamp to where a huge flock of birds had lifted into the air.

Isabella matched his gaze.

"Something spooked them," she said. "Something is out there."

Cletus, who had kept the news about Ned and JT's presence to himself to that point, raised a hand.

"I might know who that is," he said, "though I wouldn't expect them to cause a ruckus like that…"

All three of the others turned to him. Bullfinch raised an eyebrow.

"Two guys I know," he said. "Ned Peterson and John Tyler Galt. They've lived here all their lives, know as much about the swamp as any men alive. Ned sent me an e-mail this morning saying they might take a look around. There's a reward, you know, for information on the two guys who went missing."

"John Tyler Galt?" Bullfinch said. "Really?"

"Don't ask me," Cletus said, "or I'll have to shoot you. Seriously. I read the book. I assume one of his parents did too—I've never brought it up."

Isabella glanced from one to the other of them, clearly irritated. "Who is John Galt?" she asked. "And this Ned?"

Bullfinch chuckled. Cletus shook his head and turned back to the gear he'd been organizing. Jasper looked at all of them like they were crazy.

"They will either be killed," Isabella said, "or they will frighten this creature away. Either way, they have made our job harder. We need to start."

"I wouldn't count Ned or JT out that quickly," Jasper said. "They're hunters, and they're tough as stone."

Isabella said nothing.

"We're ready here," Cletus said. "Geoffrey, if you'll back the trailer up to the water?"

"With pleasure," Bullfinch said, still smiling.

A few moments later, they'd loosed the boat from the trailer and pulled the Jeep back up around the trees. Bullfinch locked it carefully and they all climbed into the sleek black fishing boat. At least, that's what it seemed to be on the surface. Once they were seated inside, and Isabella fired the powerful inboard engines, Cletus revised his initial impression.

The craft was fitted with a number of electronic devices he'd never seen before, mounted just beneath the dash and out of sight. There were cabinets and lockers beneath the seats, and mounted on the doors were several weapons, including a shotgun and two powerful hunting rifles with scopes. There were also several packs, a tent, and assorted canteens and food packs.

"I thought we were just going in for the morning?" Cletus said.

"One can never be too prepared," Bullfinch replied. "If we get on the trail, I'm not sure I could pull her off with a dozen men to help me..."

Cletus glanced up. Isabella stood with her back to them, her hands on the controls, scanning the river ahead carefully. They were moving at a slow idle, the powerful engines growling softly. He wondered just what was under the "hood". Certainly more than the Perquimans River warranted this far in toward the swamp.

The woman's movements were graceful and efficient. She seemed relaxed, but Cletus had seen that same sort of false calm in cats. They looked sleepy and quiet until something caught their attention, but it was deceptive. Beneath her calm he sensed muscles like coiled springs.

"I wouldn't want to be the thing she was hunting," he said.

Bullfinch nodded.

Jasper, who had been uncharacteristically quiet up to that point, opened his cooler and pulled out a beer. He snapped it open. Isabella glanced over her shoulder, irritated by the sound, but Jasper paid no attention. He was watching the bank on the far side of the river with more concentration than Cletus had ever seen his friend muster.

They rounded the first turn, where the two of them had been fishing.

"We were here when we heard the screams," Cletus said. "We were anchored up among those reeds."

"The other boat wasn't too far ahead," Jasper said, breaking his silence. "Don't know what will be left after the storm, but the boat was almost in the center of the channel."

Isabella nodded, but didn't turn. They rounded one corner, and then the next, and came into view of the small cove where Cletus had found the severed foot and the tracks he'd photographed.

The boat wasn't rising out of the water any longer, but they saw where Ned and JT had dragged part of it up on the shore. They also saw the other men's boat, beached and tied to a cypress formation.

"Should we go in to shore here too?" Bullfinch asked. "Would a thing like that be likely to return to the same location?"

"Believe it or not," Cletus said, "My experience with dinosaurs is limited…"

"We'll go in deeper," Isabella said. "If the two who came here ahead of us catch its attention, and they aren't immediately killed, they will lead it back this way. It would be better to come at it from the flank. Something must have driven it this close to civilization. To grow to any size without being seen, it must have kept itself deep in the swamp before now. Something has changed."

Cletus hadn't thought of that, and he frowned.

"Jasper, you ever hear any stories about anything like this before? I mean, I don't know how long a thing like that lives, or how long it takes to grow, but she's right. It didn't just spring to life big enough to smash a damned boat…"

"Not really," Jasper said. "Heard a few people tell about finding things dead deep in there, but most folks steer clear. Mostly you hear about bears or big snakes."

"Maybe some of your bears were something else entirely," Bullfinch said.

"Maybe," Jasper said. "Maybe this is the first time it came out this far. The swamp is part of a state preserve…it's big, but it butts up against agricultural land. Something could have changed in the water. Deer, they move when things aren't good where they've been, even when they've been there a long time. Maybe this thing didn't have a choice."

"You all keep saying 'thing' and 'creature,'" Cletus said. "What makes you think its mama and papa aren't out there waiting? Maybe they kicked it out of the nest?"

"I can give you some info on that," Bullfinch said. "We've tracked this thing back to around 1994—that means it's been out there for a decade or so. If what Mack uncovered is correct, it's a one-off—created in a genetic lab and let loose by a hurricane."

"Sounds like one 'a them movies on SyFy," Jasper said. "It ain't gonna get sucked up into a storm and become 'Dinocane' or something?"

"Nothing so dramatic, or unlikely," Bullfinch said. Then he glanced from Cletus to Jasper and back again, a twinkle in his eye. "If all our information is correct, though, what we're actually facing is a sort of…Crockatiel…"

Cletus turned and stared. He couldn't be certain, with the grin twitching at the edge of Bullfinch's lip, if he was shining them on, or if he just found it as funny as it sounded.

"Like one of them birds with the top-knot that never shuts up?" Jasper said. "My sister had a pair of 'em. I swear, if I thought I could do it without getting shot I'd have turned them loose out the window years ago."

"Exactly that," Bullfinch said. "Most are not aware that birds are the closest living ancestors to the dinosaurs. When our accidental mad scientists created this… thing, all that was available to them was the genetic material of a common pet bird. It's truly amazing what modern science can achieve."

"Swell," Cletus said. "We evolved from monkeys so we could

get smart enough to recreate something that died off a million years ago so it could come back and kill us. You'll pardon me if I'm not as impressed with that achievement as you seem to be."

Bullfinch's chuckle burst into a full-blown laugh. Isabella turned and glared at them, and they fell silent.

Ned brushed his fingers over a broken branch, studying it carefully. It wasn't thin like a twig. The limb was nearly the size of his forearm, and it had snapped cleanly. Whatever had passed had been big and tough. He knelt, pushing aside the brush and staring at the ground.

"No one drove through here," he said, standing.

"Look here," John Tyler said. He whistled softly.

Ned crossed to where his friend stood, and glanced down. The track was big, deep and very clear. He lifted his gaze and followed the line that whatever had made it would have to have taken. He could just make out the close end of the next track. It was a good fifteen feet away.

"Holy shit," Ned said.

"Yep," John Tyler agreed. "Damned if those idiots weren't telling the truth. Whatever made off with those two didn't carry them on an ATV."

Ned turned and stared out over the swamp to where the birds had taken flight. He pulled out a pack of Camel straights and tapped one out of the pack. He offered the pack to John Tyler, who also took one. They lit up and stood there, side by side, watching the swamp.

"We goin' after it?" John Tyler asked, finally.

"Reckon." Ned said. "Came here to do it. Not likely to sleep if we don't get it done."

John Tyler nodded. "Kind of wish I'd brought something bigger than the .30/30. Not sure I have anything big enough."

Ned laughed softly. "I go the .870 loaded with Buckshot. If this thing is fast, that will help. Don't know much about dinosaurs, but I had an uncle who hunted gators. They have soft spots, and you can go for the eyes."

John Tyler nodded again.

"Maybe it won't come to that. We don't have to kill it—today. We just need something to prove the damn thing is out here, and that it's what took them boys off their boat. This is one time I won't mind lettin' ol Sheriff Bob get the glory."

They fell silent and finished their smokes, then crushed out the butts in the loamy ground and started off on the wide, crushed trail. There wasn't going to be much tracking involved, unless it hit another patch of water. They moved as quickly and silently as possible. They had a lot of experience with the swamp, but both of them knew they'd stepped out of their depth the minute they saw the broken tree limb.

They followed for another quarter of a mile before John Tyler reached out an arm and stopped his friend. He pointed with the tip of his rifle. There was a swatch of flannel hanging off the limb of a cypress branch just ahead. When they moved in closer, they saw it was crusted with dried blood. John Tyler pulled it free and tucked it into his hip pocket.

Neither man spoke. The swamp was very, very still. There were two things that meant trouble in The Great Dismal. One was a ruckus—like the birds taking flight, or deer and smaller game taking off suddenly. The other was dead silence. Whatever creatures were close enough that they couldn't escape whatever they sensed grew silent. They stilled their breath. They did not rustle in the brush or cause ripples in the water. They sat, and they waited. That silence had fallen all around them, and neither man wanted to be the first to break it.

There was a soft splashing sound off to the right. Ned turned slowly. John Tyler was already facing in the direction of the sound. He brought the rifle very slowly up to his shoulder. Ned backed toward his friend, swinging the shotgun up and around.

The sound repeated, followed by a soft slosh.

Ned took a very slow step forward. There was a stand of cypress between the two of them, and whatever was making that sound. It didn't sound large, but there was no way to know what the movement meant. Could be a snake, or a fish—anything. Or it could be one small motion from a much larger creature.

"The belly," Ned whispered, stepping forward. "Don't forget. If you get a shot—the eyes or the belly."

He reached the cypress tree, hesitated only for a moment, and then used the rifle barrel to brush the leaves apart.

At first, neither man could make out a thing. They saw daylight through the branches, but nothing moved. Ned pushed the brush a little farther to the side and stepped around to one side. John Tyler circled to the other side.

They saw the deer at the same moment. It was a young buck, and it twitched nervously hearing their approach. It's muscles tensed, and it half turned, head cocked to one side. Ned started to lower the barrel of the rifle in relief—and then the swamp exploded with sound.

The buck sprang, but it was far too slow. Massive jaws rose from the shadows behind it, snapping closed with a hideous crunch that nearly cut that animal in two. Ned stumbled back, tripped, and his finger hit the trigger. The gun's report echoed wildly through the swamp.

John Tyler didn't hesitate. As the thing rose up and kept rising, he aimed, and when those massive jaws ground down on the deer, he fired. The shotgun blast caught the thing under the chin. It reared, dropping the deer and shaking its head. He fired again, but the second shot hit it on the side. It seemed to glance off, no more than scratching skin.

Ned grabbed his arm as he raised the shotgun a third time.

"We got to go," Ned said. "If that didn't kill it, you ain't going to kill it."

John Tyler fought to free his arm, but Ned yanked harder.

"Damn it, John Tyler," Ned said. "Run!"

At that second, the beast let out an ear-splitting roar. It reared up again, shaking its head from side to side. It was hurt, but not seriously. Any moment it would regain its equilibrium and start looking for whatever had caused it pain. John Tyler stared at it another long moment, then turned, and the two of them tore out through the swamp. They didn't look back, there was no point. It was following—or it wasn't—but their only hope was in forward motion and blind luck.

They retraced their route from the river, moving as quickly as the mud, gnarled roots, and trees would allow.

"Christ on a stick!" Ned said. "What in blue hell was that?"

"Big," John Tyler said. "Holy Christ…"

There was another scream behind them, but farther away and muffled by the damp, heavy air.

"Don't think it's coming," Ned said.

"Didn't think it was there before," John Tyler said. "Not taking any chances. Carry your ass."

They continued in silence. When they passed through the broken branches that had ushered them into the swamp and onto the riverbank, they dove for their boat and shoved it into the river. Ned had the motor revved almost before they hit the channel.

"Jesus," John Tyler said. "Be careful. You hit that prop on a log and we'll be rowing our asses out of here."

Then the two of them were in the boat. Ned brought it around in a sharp turn, and they tore back up the river. The wake from their passing rolled up and over the bank on either side. Only a few moments later, the river was calm again, and the two men were out of sight.

"Did you hear that?" Cletus said. "That was a gunshot…"

Isabella turned and glared at him. Even Jasper turned and grinned.

"Okay, okay," Cletus said. "You heard. That had to be Ned and J. T. If they're out there shooting…"

"Then they are probably dead," Isabella said. She turned the boat sharply toward the bank.

"Hey!" Jasper cried out. He nearly spun off his seat, holding his beer over his head and sloshing foam over the side.

Isabella killed the engine. The bow of the boat slid softly up onto the bank, and she was up and moving before it came to a halt, hauling a heavy line behind her and wrapping it around a cypress.

"Hold your horses, lady," Cletus said.

"There is no time for talk," she said. "If we move quickly, we may be able to save your friends. If it gets away, we will have to track it into the swamp…"

"I ain't trackin' nothin' through the swamp," Jasper said, glaring at her. "You're flat crazy…"

"Fine," Isabella said. "You can wait here. Alone."

She climbed back onto the boat and started grabbing her gear— a very high-powered rifle, a handgun, and one of the four packs. Bullfinch was moving as well, sliding the straps of a second pack over his shoulders.

"It *is* why we came here," he said, shrugging his shoulders apologetically. "We have to go in after your friends. We'll discuss further tracking if it should prove necessary."

Cletus sighed and rose. He picked up one of the remaining packs, shouldered a shotgun and hopped to the bank. Jasper sat for a moment longer, staring at his friend. When Cletus turned to follow the other two into the swamp, Jasper rose in a lurch, nearly tumbled off the side of the boat, and cursed. He grabbed the last pack and another shotgun. He started to follow, then thought better of it. He dropped his empty into his cooler and fished out a fresh beer. With that in hand, he clambered onto the bank and hurried after Cletus' receding back.

Somewhere ahead, something very big, and very angry, screamed.

16

Mack double-checked the address he'd plugged into his GPS. He was in a rental car, but he always carried his own tech. It was more reliable, and generations more complex, and it kept him connected to the labyrinthine forest of cables and monitors in Colorado and his own network in Arizona. In the trunk he had a workstation he could set up and break down rapidly that gave him full access and control, but for the moment it was enough to drive, and monitor.

Samuel Montgomery and his now wife, Beatrice owned a home outside Raleigh, North Carolina. They also owned a small chain of DNA labs throughout the state, performing the same sort of function as the lab they'd shared outside Old Mill, though with contracts Mack had traced to government projects and the FBI.

Their professional life had been easy to trace, but the information he really needed had proven a great deal more obscure. After running a blog for a number of years where Beatrice had reported on the incidents surrounding hurricane Callie, and the destruction of their lab and their experiments, the two had faded into the anonymity of normalcy. Probably they had realized no one was likely to take them seriously without proof, and without a direct link back to Eddie Dodd, who'd sent in the original sample, they had no way to duplicate their effort. It would have been professional suicide to continue pushing a cryptozoological agenda publicly. He only hoped they'd continued their interest off the grid.

He was willing to bet that they had. The fact that they had not only continued their work in the field of DNA, but expanded it in directions that might grant access to less mundane tasks than sexing birds and tracing the genealogical roots of prize poodles was an indicator.

Mack was no stranger to such interests. His own research covered nearly every occult and obscure conspiracy theory ever recorded, along with reports of alien abductions, crashed space ships, and extra-sensory perception. It was that obsessive information gathering that had led to the network behind O.C.L.T. and, over time, to this particular visit.

As he wound up into the mountains, he thought how odd it was that these two lived here, so close to Rebecca York's estate, and yet he'd never before made a connection, despite the oddities of the Montgomerys' blog posts. He couldn't help but go over the algorithms that bound his searches as he drove, trying to see what might have excluded this particular anomaly, and how to adjust for it.

Mack's network went far beyond anything resembling the Internet so many have come to love or loathe. His was the intellect behind some of the most intricate security software in the world. He maintained that security for a wide variety of clients, some within, and some beyond the scope of the O.C.L.T. He had backdoors and searchbots in every crack and crevice of the digital world, and in some that only existed because of bridges he'd created. He had developed complex alerts and cross-linking programs to tie theoretically unrelated things together into coherent data.

Bullfinch claimed that he had gone beyond the world of tech, as it was known, into some sort of quantum, almost supernatural link connecting (very literally) the known world. Mack didn't really care what they called it—it was what he did. He also enjoyed extreme sports, distance running (as long as he was fully Wi-Fi connected while off the main grid), skydiving, and a number of other unlikely hobbies. Dinosaurs, as it turned out, were one of his favorite fascinations.

He heard a soft chime and glanced down at his monitor. He'd received another hit from the Old Mill, North Carolina, area that his system deemed relevant. He pulled over and began punching buttons on a tiny Bluetooth keyboard.

It seemed there were a couple of local experts in the field of fossils and ancient reptiles living very near where Bullfinch and Isabella had begun their hunt. He brought up the contact information, scanned it, and sent two quick notes. The first was to Bullfinch, alerting him to the possibility of contact due to the second.

The second went to a Mr. Al Seidel, and his friend and associate Jim Cross, founding members of what appeared to be a very obscure organization, the Acheulean Society... Mack knew that the earliest-known tools discovered from the worlds of early man were the Acheulean Axes... He wished he had time for more research. He typed quickly:

> *Mr. Seidel, and Mr. Cross,*
>
> *This is going to sound odd any way I write it, so I'll come straight to the point. Two of my associates are in your area. We have reason to believe that a creature, a reptile that should have perished millions of years ago, has been spotted, and has killed in the swamp near Old Mill, NC.*
> *I understand you have extensive knowledge of creatures of the proper period, Early Cretaceous, and have research materials you might be willing to spare. I hope you won't mind that I've forwarded your contact information.*
>
> *Wendell Macklemore*
>
> *O.C.L.T.*

He hit *Send*. He knew he wasn't supposed to directly acknowledge the O.C.L.T. in such a correspondence, but he also knew that if he didn't trust his own judgment, most of his e-mails and contacts would be ignored. While not so many people believed in the supernatural or strange, a great number believed in secret organizations and government secrets. It was better to hook them with the latter and break the news of the former more slowly. He also knew that the powers that cared about their discretion were focused on terrorism, espionage, big business, and a thousand other key terms and specific criteria, none of which involved dinosaurs or the Early Cretaceous Period. The odds of his message being intercepted or flagged were minimal. They were lessened further by the fact he was the one who'd set up the filters that would have flagged it. Sometimes it was good to be the geek.

He pulled into the driveway of a one-story ranch home near the top of a ridge. There were two vehicles in the drive—an old beat up Jeep and a station wagon. Mack pulled in behind the Jeep and gathered his thoughts. He took a last look at his monitors, checked a couple of incoming messages, and killed the engine.

He climbed out and made his way to the door. His ring was answered after only a few moments by a tall, attractive woman. She had long, dark hair, pulled back in a ponytail, and she was dressed in shorts and running shoes.

"Yes?" she said.

"Beatrice Montgomery?" Max asked. "My name is Wendell Macklemore. My friends call me Mack... I'd like to speak with you for a moment, if you have the time?"

"I was just on my way out for a run," she said, hesitating. "What is this about?"

"I was wondering," Mack said, watching her face carefully, "if you might have information on a Sarcosuchus?"

Her eyes grew wide, and she covered her mouth with one hand.

Mack added, "There seems to be one killing people near Old Mill... I thought maybe you and Samuel would be interested..."

"Come in," she said. "Oh God, are you *kidding* me? Come in. Sammy is out back. I'll call him..."

"Thanks," Mack said. He stepped inside, and waited as Beatrice disappeared down a hallway that ran all the way to another larger door at the rear of the home. She slammed through it and was gone before Mack even had the front door closed behind him.

A few moments later, she returned. A man followed on her heels. Samuel Montgomery was slightly older than his wife, thin with a beak for a nose, but he'd put on weight since the images Mack had found online. His skin was tanned, and he was leanly muscled. A runner's build.

"What is this?" he said. His eyes were animated, darting to Mack, past him, around the room and back, as if he had so much energy he couldn't burn it quickly enough. "What is this about a Sarchosuchus? I assure you, young man, that if this is some sort of joke after all these years, it's in exceedingly poor taste."

Mack held out his hand.

"No joke, I assure you," he said. "The organization that employs me has a history of becoming embroiled in… odd situations. I introduced myself to Mrs. Montgomery already. My name is Mack, and I really hope you might be able to help me with some background…"

"Is it possible?" Beatrice asked, tugging on Samuel's shoulder. "After all these years. How?"

Mack reached into his pocket and pulled out a folded newspaper article from *The Daily Advance*, the local paper out of Elizabeth City, North Carolina. Samuel scanned it and then handed it to Beatrice.

"This is hardly conclusive," Samuel said.

"My people are already on the scene," Mack said. "Early reports confirm that something very large attacked and killed at least one man. Two are missing. There were photos taken of prints at the scene. They were later wiped out by a storm, so there are no corroborating shots, but they are very clear, and the photographer, one Cletus Diggs, had the forethought to provide perspective on the shot. They were big, and they fit what is known of Sarchosuchus. My own work uncovered your blog. We actually located Mr. Dodd, the man who provided your original sample. He had a very… interesting tale to tell. I believe your identification was very close. I think what we have on our hands is actually a Fasolasuchus, a little more upright."

"I tried to contact him for years," Beatrice said. "I could never find him, or, if I did find him he didn't admit to being *the* Eddie Dodd who collected that sample."

"He saw something in South America that frightened him very badly," Mack said. "He didn't want anything to do with it, and was afraid someone would try to enlist his aid in going back down there. He thought the government might have found a way to force him. I can tell you that, as interesting as his encounter might have been, he has no desire to or intention of repeating it."

Mack ran down Dodd's experience in the jungle, the battle he'd witnessed between the tiger and the creature he'd taken his sample from.

"He didn't know a thing about dinosaurs," Mack said. "He just knew it was big, and that it should not have been there."

"That much we all agree on," Samuel said. "The damned things have been extinct for centuries ... or so we believed. Those are deep jungles, and it's always possible something that has been hidden away for a very long time was forced out of hiding by changing environment or new circumstances..."

"That's what we believe is happening in North Carolina, as well," Mack said. "For the creature to be the size we are certain that it is, it has to have existed in the depths of The Great Dismal for at least a decade, and even then the growth curve would have to be phenomenal."

"There are theories," Beatrice said. "The so-called 'Super Crocs' are among the only creatures of any era that continue growing throughout the span of their life. Many believe that growth was abnormally quick, enabling young adults to reach a size and strength that allowed them to preserve their lives in a world filled with predators we can only imagine."

"This is fascinating," Samuel cut in, "and I understand you are being thorough, coming here to question us, but let me ask you this. What can we do? You can't just dump this on us, tip your cap, and disappear. I mean, sure, we may have started this by accident—or by act of God, more accurately—but *Jesus*, we have *got* to know what happens to this thing. Will they kill it? Are they going to try and capture it? Contain it? Will your people be contacting the press?"

"That's a whole lot of questions," Mack replied. "I"m authorized to fly you down there to be part of the operation. We can use any expertise available, even though you have no direct contact with such a creature. The operation is strictly confidential. Even if they manage to contain it without killing it—our agents on the scene are divided evenly on that issue—I'm pretty certain it will be kept 'underground.' We assume it's the only one of its kind, but in case it's not…. All of us have seen *Jurassic Park*, after all, we'll need more information before we can release what we have publicly. That swamp would be full of amateur dinosaur hunters in an hour of any report we might release, and the likelihood is either a lot of them would end up hurt, or killed, or they'd interfere with our own efforts. In that case, Isabella—you'll meet her if you accompany me—might kill them herself."

"This is a lot to take in," Samuel said.

"I'll get started packing," Beatrice said, turning and crossing the room without a glance back at either of them.

The two men stared as she departed, then, as if on cue, started laughing.

"I guess that settles that," Samuel said. "There's one more thing though, and I don't know if, or how, it might be important, but we own the bird."

"The bird?"

"'The' Bird," Samuel said, nodding. "Tiki. Tiki Kowalski the Cockatiel whose DNA we used back then. He's an old fellow now, but if what you are telling me is true, he's some sort of step-parent to that thing in the swamp."

"But how…"

"We tracked him down," Samuel said. As he talked, he led Mack into another room. There were several cages lining the walls with a number of large, attractively colored birds. In the back corner, near a black grand piano, stood another cage a little bit separated from the others.

"He's not very sociable with the other birds," Samuel said. "Ever since his buddy Gypsy died a couple of years back, he's preferred his solitude, except for when we take him out. When we found him, the previous owners were tired of the noise. He has a little song and dance that can go on a long time, and he's not shy about it. We bought him, and he's been with us ever since."

Samuel opened the cage door and stuck his hand inside. The bird, a flash of gray and white feathers topped by a shock of bright yellow hair, pecked at him and squawked. The bird backed away half a step. Unperturbed, Samuel pressed his finger into the bird's stomach, and it stepped up onto his finger. He drew the hand out, and the Cockatiel glared at Mack as if whatever was happening was surely his fault.

"Tiki, meet Mack," Samuel chuckled. "Mack, meet the grumpiest Cockatiel this side of South America, Tiki Kowalski."

"Doesn't look Polish," Mack said, and grinned.

"Named after some penguin," Samuel said. "Never quite understood it, but the name seems to fit. We played around with changing it over the years, but it stuck."

"Isn't he pretty old?" Mack asked.

Beatrice entered the room then.

"They can live more than twenty years, so I guess he's middle-aged. His companion died young. We never really figured out what happened. It took Tiki a long time to get his song back after that."

"Song," Samuel muttered. "Hardly."

Beatrice held out a hand and Tiki lifted off from Samuel's finger and flew over to land on her head. He walked in a circle, looking irritated. They all laughed.

"Anyway," Samuel said, "I'm not sure why, but I have the sense that we may want Tiki to tag along. There is some sort of bond, however slight and tenuous, between him and that creature. He may prove useful, though I can't imagine how."

"I'm not opposed," Mack said. "As long as he can take a flight that isn't under his own power… You'll have to be responsible for him once we land. I might not be sticking around, and our team is in the field… When they return they probably won't be in much of a mood to socialize."

"Of course," Beatrice said. "Tiki is pretty self-sufficient, as long as there's plenty of birdseed."

The bird, as if sensing he had become the center of attention, dipped his head, almost as if bowing, and began an odd shuffling step across Beatrice's head. As he moved, he began to whistle, a repetitious tune ending in several sharp whistles, each pass on the tune ending with another dipping bow as he crisscrossed Beatrice's skull.

"And… there it is," Samuel said. "We call it the 'Tiki Tango,' or 'Chirpin' the bird.' It's not likely to catch on on the pop charts."

Mack laughed. On an impulse, he held out his finger to the dancing bird. Tiki glanced at him, looked as if he might bite, and then hopped onto the finger with a flutter of his feathers. He sat there, glaring at Mack, who studied him in return, fascinated.

"I've never held a bird before," he said.

"Tiki doesn't cuddle, like some birds," Beatrice said, "but he's a good companion. Pretty smart, too, when he wants to be. I'm frankly surprised he came to you. He's grumpy enough with us. Hates most of the other birds, and I'm pretty sure he still misses his friend."

Mack studied the bird, and nodded. "We all have things we've lost," he said. "I guess it's no different for a bird."

Beatrice laughed and took Tiki back, returning him to his cage. "Everything is different for a bird," she said. "Humans are always acting like their pets reactions and emotions are somehow extensions of their own. "It's enough that, despite the absolute differences between species, we find connections. I think you may have just found one…he's still watching you."

"I'll get the travel cage," Samuel said.

Mack watched the bird for a few more minutes. He reached out to the edge of the cage, but Tiki snapped at his finger. The bird could have latched on, but it didn't. It was more a warning, or… something? Mack grinned.

"I think we're going to be buddies," he said. Then he leaned in closer to the cage. "Just between you and me, I *know* who Kowalski was. You can call me Skipper…"

He turned and saw Beatrice watching him strangely. He smiled at her. "I'll go get the trunk open. I'll call ahead and have the jet ready."

They both left the room. Mack headed for the door and the car and Beatrice finished her rapid packing. Standing on the perch in the center of his cage, Tiki watched until the two humans were out of sight, then turned and began slowly preening his tail feathers.

17

Once she started moving, Isabella was fast and relentless. She pulled ahead of the others repeatedly, hesitating only reluctantly when Bullfinch called out to her. She would have gone on, but the noise they made crashing after her and calling for her to wait was dangerous.

"Jesus," Jasper said. "This here's a swamp, not a racetrack."

"The creature is not slow," Isabella said.

"How do you know that?" Cletus asked. He studied the ground around them. So far he'd seen no sign of a trail, and from experience he knew that whatever they were chasing wasn't likely to pass unnoticed.

Isabella glanced toward the sky, and nodded.

Ahead, another flock of birds lifted off.

"Your friends are either dead or on their way out of the swamp. Whatever spooked the birds is about a half-mile away. It was only a quarter-mile the last time this happened."

"We'll never catch it at that pace," Bullfinch said.

"We don't know that it will continue running," Isabella said. "We have to find the trail. Once we can track its movements, we'll know more."

"How in *hell* did you watch for double-d-goddam *birds* and still keep movin' so fast?" Jasper said.

"Fast?" Isabella raised an eyebrow. "I would have caught up with it by now on my own. We are not moving fast. Not fast enough. If we lose it, we may not get another chance like this one.

We know it's on the move. I think it may be hurt."

"The gunshots?" Bullfinch asked.

She nodded. "I don't believe a creature like this would move so far so fast without reason. It's trying to distance itself from whatever caused it pain. It needs to feed, and to rest. If we can find the trail and keep moving, I believe we will run it down."

"That's likely to be more difficult than you think," Cletus said. "So far, we're on the outskirts. There's plenty of dry ground here. Once you move in deeper, it's rougher going. A lot of it's water, and one advantage that thing has is it can cross whatever it comes up against. We have to find ways around, or through. If we don't find it before long, we're going to have come up with a different plan."

Isabella turned without a word and started off through the cypress and brush. Cletus glanced at Jasper, who shrugged. Bullfinch was already headed off in pursuit.

"She'll see soon enough," Jasper said. "Ain't no quick way through here for a man, or a crazy woman. She might be good at huntin' big uglies, but she doesn't know everything."

They followed as close behind Bullfinch as they could. Isabella bobbed in and out of sight as she swung over and around trees, dipping easily through holes that seemed too small to accommodate a dog, let alone a human. She had an uncanny sense of direction, and the few times the others paused, they heard no sound at her passing.

After about fifteen minutes of this, she suddenly came to a halt. Bullfinch stepped up behind her, and saw that she was staring out over a dark, moss-clotted expanse of water. Cypress knees and logs stuck up out of the muck here and there, but nothing dry. There were hillocks and small islands of muck circling around the water to either side, but it was unclear if they continued in a straight line to either side, or wound around toward where yet another flock of birds, very far away, had just taken flight.

Isabella didn't speak. Bullfinch, feeling the weight of the silence, cursed.

"Damn it all," he said.

"Hate to say 'I told you so,' you know?" Jasper said, "But…"

Cletus scanned the edge of the water and grew very still.

"Isabella," he said. "Don't move."

She almost turned. She almost glanced his way, but did not. Her training was deeply ingrained, and though she was irritated, and not particularly impressed with her companion's skills, she sensed the danger in his voice.

Cletus very slowly raised the barrel of the shotgun. His hand trembled slightly, and he took a deep breath. He remembered what his father had told him so far in the past it came to him only like snatches of bad dreams.

"You hold it steady, boy. Time enough to think about what you're shootin' after it's dead and twitchin'—you don't hesitate on the near side of pulling the trigger if you want to grow old and mean like me."

A dark V spread out, maybe a foot from Isabella's ankle. The moccasin had raised its head from the water, swaying only slightly. There was no hesitation on its part. It was aggressive, a predator, and they had invaded its territory. Probably they were too near its nest. Might be eggs, or young.

Cletus inhaled, held the breath, and fired. The shotgun was loud in the near total silence of the moment.

At the sound, Isabella moved. She was fast, possibly faster than the snake would have been. The buckshot blew the top half of the snake into bits, splattering it back across the water.

"Jesus," Jasper said. "What the hell?"

"There are going to be more," Cletus said. "They nest. We're too close. Keep your eyes open."

Isabella still said nothing, but she glanced at Cletus with something akin to respect.

"We're not going to catch it," Bullfinch said. "Not now. Even if there was a way across, or around this … whatever it is," he gestured at the expanse of dark water, "it's going to have heard the gunshot. If your friends," he glanced at Cletus, "actually managed to hurt it, it's going to associate the sound."

Isabella pulled out her phone. She tapped on the screen rapidly, and then turned to face them.

"I have asked for Mack to get surveillance as quickly as possible, and for an aerial survey of the area. We're going to need a good map so this won't happen again, and different equipment. If we had brought in a raft..."

Bullfinch nodded.

"So," Cletus said, "we're going back?"

"Yes," Isabella said. "We need to find the two who were here before we arrived. The two who chased it off. They must have seen it. We need to question them, and we need to regroup."

Her phone vibrated, and she pulled it out.

A moment later, she tucked it into its holster and turned, heading back through the brush toward the river.

"Mack will be here this evening," she said. "He's bringing someone with him. He says it's important. The survey of the area is already underway."

"All I know," Jasper said, falling in at the back of the group and keeping his eyes peeled for snakes, "is I'm ready for another beer."

They headed off through the brush at a fast walk. Far behind them, almost out of sight, another flock of birds took flight.

They moved in silence back toward the river and their boat. With the imminent threat removed, they paid less attention to what they passed. Jasper kept an eye out for snakes, but that meant he wasn't watching the trees. They stepped into the clearing, face to face with the bear, before any of them realized the danger.

It was a black bear, an old one. When it saw them, it reared up, a good six-and-a-half feet of angry fur and deadly claws. Cletus was near the back of the group. He couldn't get a shot, because the others all stood in his line of sight. Jasper was nursing the last of the beer he'd carried in, and Bullfinch was so startled he almost dropped his gun in his haste to lift it and aim.

Only Isabella was unfazed. She met the bear's gaze, dropped into a crouch, and sprang. One moment she and the animal faced one another, and the next she'd catapulted to a lower branch on one of the trees overhead, tucked her long legs, and soared into the air.

The bear was as startled as they were. It roared, swung at Isabella with deadly speed, and missed. Cletus, realizing the danger, began screaming and waving his arms, dancing like a fool to distract the animal. The bear was confused, but only momentarily. Confronted by a number of threats, it chose the closest, Bullfinch, and lunged.

Cletus raised his shotgun, ready to chance a shot if he got half an opening. He never had a chance to get that shot off. Isabella, who had swung up into the tree and out of sight, suddenly reappeared. She dropped down behind the bear and shouted at it. The beast stopped again, confused. It spun, swiping at her with one great paw. Isabella dodged the attack, leaped, and actually did a flip over the animal's head. As she passed, her arm shot down, and she jabbed at its shoulder. Then she was over and down, rolling back and away seconds before the bear's swiping claw could remove chunks of her flesh.

"What the hell was that?" Cletus asked, raising his gun

Isabella reached out and placed her palm on top of the barrel, lowering it to the ground. Cletus glanced at her, and then back at the bear.

It staggered. It turned toward Jasper, took a step, then one of its legs buckled, and it toppled to the side. Jasper jumped back, and the bear dropped to the ground.

They all stood very still for a long moment, then Bullfinch stepped forward and prodded the bear with the barrel of his gun. It didn't move.

"It will be out for at least twenty minutes," Isabella said. "I dosed it with a tranquilizer."

"That you just happened to have in your hand when you flew up into that tree?" Jasper said. He was staring openly. "You looked like a damn superhero. Why didn't you tell us you could fly?"

Isabella stared at him for a moment, then she smiled.

"You didn't ask," she said. Then, "I pulled the tranquilizer out of my belt when I was in the tree. This creature has done nothing to hurt us, or anyone else. It will sleep, and then it will wake. It will probably not even remember we were here."

"I'll remember for it," Cletus said. "That was pretty damned awesome."

Isabella shrugged. She turned, and without another word, started off through the swamp toward the river. The others fell in behind her. Cletus glanced at Bullfinch, who shrugged and smiled.

"I told you she was a hunter, Cletus," he said. "I might have left out the superhero part…"

Cletus shook his head and grinned. He suddenly felt a little better about their odds of surviving the week.

18

The boat was back on the trailer, and they were rolling slowly down the old dirt road toward Highway 17. Cletus was on his phone. He'd managed to get through to Ned and, relaying comments back and forth between Bullfinch, who was on his own phone with Mack, and Isabella, who was irritable and full of nervous energy, he managed to set up a meeting for later that evening.

"I'm going to call down to the Cotton Gin and reserve the back room," he said. "My trailer's too small, and if we all invade Jasper's place, his ol' Pap will skin us alive. Probably going to be glued to the race tonight, and I don't want to be the one who has to deny it to him. We can get food and circle the wagons."

"What wagons?" Isabella snapped. "What are you talking about?"

"It's an expression," Bullfinch said. "We'll get our plan set, see what kind of information Mack has come up with, and get all our 'ducks in a row,' to use a local colloquialism.

"I believe there are at least two others who should be present, if possible. Mack sent me contact information for two local men, amateur anthropologists, collectors of the strange, and particularly knowledgeable in the realm of fossils and dinosaurs. They have some materials that may prove helpful."

"The more the merrier," Cletus said. "This is turning into a circus already. Might as well warn you all up front, Ned and John Tyler—they aren't exactly social butterflies. They don't get out much, and when they do they mostly keep to themselves. This is likely to be a little outside their comfort zone. Add that to the fact they faced off with a double-d goddam dinosaur earlier today, and I can't guarantee their good humor."

"There are too many involved," Isabella said. "This should be kept quiet. We should be handling this as secretly as possible, and now we have, as you say, a circus. If too much information reaches others in the community, there will be hunters all over the swamp."

"I tell you one thing," Jasper said. "If Ned and J. T. say they took off with their tails between their legs, you won't have to worry too much about anyone else local. If they can't track it through that swamp and kill it, there aren't many others going to even try. Probably work in your favor if they *do* talk."

"Don't you mean *our* favor?" Cletus said.

Jasper glared at him. "I didn't say it would stop idjits," he muttered.

When they pulled into the driveway of the bed and breakfast, Cletus and Jasper climbed out. Cletus gave Bullfinch directions to the Cotton Gin, and they agreed to take a couple of hours to clean up and give the others they were meeting with a chance to get cleaned up.

There was a dark blue SUV parked in the lot. It had rental tags.

"Looks like Mack is here," Bullfinch said. "I'll fill him in."

Cletus nodded. "Good. I want to get some of this mud off of me. We'll see you all later. I'm going to swing by and let Bob, the local sheriff, know what we're doing. He probably won't want anything to do with it, but if things go badly, I don't want him coming to me later and asking why I didn't mention we were out in the swamp chasing his dinosaur."

"I'm surprised he wasn't out there with those troopers again," Jasper said. "They probably decided Cletus is crazy, and that those two idjits took off through the swamp on their own. They'll write it off as a missing person… no way he's traipsing through that swamp. He'll probably tell us 'Go with God but don't expect him answerin' your prayers,' or something equally useless."

"Probably," Cletus said. "Still, if we go out there and you get your head bit off by a prehistoric crocodile, I want to be able to say

'I told you so' when he has to fill out all the paperwork."

Jasper frowned and dragged his cooler out of the boat.

"Keep laughin' and I'll be home watching that race with pap."

Cletus laughed. They carried the beer to his truck and turned back toward the highway. The sun was just starting to drop toward the trees.

The Cotton Gin was hopping, but Cletus drove on through the gathered pickup trucks, old-school muscle cars and beaters to the service drive that ran around to the back of the building. Jasper had, reluctantly, left the cooler of beer at home, and was already staring longingly at the back door of the club.

Ned and John Tyler were waiting in their truck. Cletus pulled in beside them, and he and Jasper climbed out. Ned nodded and stepped down. John Tyler followed suit.

"Let's get inside," Jasper said. "I'm hungry, and I'm thirsty."

"You go on ahead, Jaz," Cletus said. "Order some pitchers and get us situated. I'm gonna talk to Ned here, and then I'll wait for the others. None of them has been back here, except maybe that Seidel guy, and I don't know him. Don't want anyone getting lost."

Jasper didn't say a word. He headed for the back door to the Gin and on through. John Tyler nodded at Cletus, and then followed. Cletus turned and stared out over the cotton field behind the club, waiting to see if Ned would speak first.

"We saw it," Ned said finally. "Pretty sure we shot it. Had a plan, try to hit it underneath, maybe a belly shot, or the throat. Damn thing… "

"What?" Cletus asked. He didn't turn, not wanting to interrupt.

"It's big, Cletus," Ned said. "Bigger than I could have imagined. I know we hit it, but I don't know if I hurt it. We confused it, and we got the hell out. Pretty sure if we hadn't, we wouldn't be talkin' now. Never ran from a damn thing in my life, but I'm here tell you I was scootin' across that swamp."

"Hell, Ned, it wasn't like it was a bear, or even a regular damned crocodile. What in hell else could you have done?"

"I know, Cletus, but here's the thing. I live in that swamp. I'm out there every day, and now I know—that thing is out there too. You know what I'm sayin'?"

"I do," Cletus said. "My trailer ain't that far from the swamp. Here's the thing—these folks that are here to help? They aren't playing around. This is the sort of thing they do. Believe it or not, a damn dinosaur in the swamp isn't the craziest thing to happen, even around here. I know. You tell them what you saw, and what you know. They'll get it, one way or the other."

"Hope you're right," Ned said. "Gonna be damned hard to sleep tonight."

The silence was broken by the crunch of tires on gravel. The blue SUV rounded the corner, and Cletus saw it was packed. Bullfinch was driving, and Isabella had shotgun. In the back, a couple he'd never seen before sat in the first row of bucket seats. In the far back was one more passenger, who had his arm around something large, but not large enough to be another person.

Bullfinch parked alongside Cletus' truck, and they all piled out.

"Cletus," Bullfinch said. "One of these days we have to meet when there's no emergency on the line. I have heard some stories that I'd love to get your side of..."

"I can say the same," Cletus said, taking the man's hand and grinning.

Bullfinch turned, and nodded at his companions. "You know Isabella. The two beside her are Samuel and Beatrice Montgomery, geneticists and probably creators of our reptilian friend."

Behind them all, a tall, athletic man stood grinning. In one hand he held a good-sized bird cage. On the perch inside, shuffling back and forth and glaring at them all, was a big gray Cockatiel with a yellow shock of feathers on top of his head.

"And your bird-loving friend?" Cletus said.

"That would be Mack," Bullfinch said. "You've met online, I understand, but this is the computer genius in the flesh. The bird is known as Tiki Kowalski. Oddly, he's the closest living relative to the thing we're tracking."

"But...why'd you bring it here?" Ned asked, breaking his silence and staring openly.

Mack stepped up. "Well, he wasn't too happy when we started to leave the room, and we were afraid if we left him there squawking we'd find our luggage on the lawn when we got back. I figured since he was involved in this from the beginning, might as well bring him along."

Cletus was about to say something when the sound of another engine broke the silence. They all turned as an odd contraption rounded the corner. It was a motorcycle, or it seemed to be. It had two wheels in the front and one in back. It was low-slung, and looked like a rocket on wheels. Astride it, curls of hair sneaking out from beneath a solid black helmet, a red-faced man in a pink polo shirt wheeled around the corner at about twice the legal speed. He saw them, circled around, and came to a sliding stop on the far side of the SUV.

As he turned off his bike and unhooked his helmet, Bullfinch approached him.

"Mr. Seidel?" he said.

The man smiled and held out his hand.

"Al. You must be Bullfinch."

"As charged," Bullfinch said, shaking. "We really appreciate your assistance. I wasn't able to bring much along in the way of reference materials, and this is a little outside my area of expertise."

"You tell me there's a dinosaur running around the swamp down by Hertford, and it's outside your area of expertise?" Seidel said. "Whose area of expertise would that fall *inside* of?"

"My research says that, around these parts, if it's anyone, it's you," Mack said. He managed to shake hands despite the birdcage. "Mr. Cross couldn't make it?"

"He's out of town. Jim is tracking something down for me. I collect… artifacts. Just about now he should be driving into South Dakota."

"I know a little about your collection," Mack said. "Word has it you have an actual Mammoth tusk…"

"I have Mastodon tusks too," he said, grinning. "Acheulean axes, trilobites. I'm interested in where we all came from—what makes the world tick."

"You're gonna love this then," Ned said. "Let's get inside and get some of that beer."

They turned as a group and headed for the back door of the Cotton Gin. Cletus hurried ahead and held the door for Isabella first, then the others. They entered a large, mostly open room. In the center were several round tables. The room was rented occasionally for parties and meetings. Right now it was empty except for their group. Jasper and John Tyler sat at a long table. There were bowls in the center, filled with corn chips and peanuts. Several pitchers of beer and a small army of empty glasses sat beside the food.

"We are wasting time," Isabella said. She did not take a seat at the table, and she eyed the beer with disapproval.

"Patience," Bullfinch said. "There is a lot more to this story than we first believed, and our expedition this morning has convinced me that, at the least, we have some work to do to prepare before we go back in. Everyone here holds a small piece of the puzzle…"

At that moment, Tiki let out a chirping whistle. Bullfinch turned, startled, and then began to laugh.

"Well, yes, even you my friend," he said. "I suggest we start as close to the beginning as possible. Mack can tell us what he learned of a certain Mr. Dodd, who is responsible for discovering the original DNA sample that led to… well, to here. From there, I believe Samuel and Beatrice can fill in more details, and then we'll get down to actual planning. Ned and John Tyler have actually *seen* this thing. Confronted it. Mr. Seidel…"

"Al," the man said. "Call me Al."

"Al…" Bullfinch continued, "has some materials with him concerning the particular species of theoretically extinct creature we are dealing with. We have aerial maps, and it is just possible we can figure out where our crockatiel has been hiding all these years, why it is no longer doing so, and what to do about it."

"Sounds reasonable to me," Cletus said. "To keep things at the level of full disclosure, I contacted the local sheriff and told him what we were doing. He and the State Police have written this off— for now. Bob, he knows crazy things happen here, and I'm sure he knows there's more to it than meets the eye, but the evidence they were able to find after the storm has not led the State Police to believe there is more here than a couple of missing fishermen. No one else is planning on going into the swamp—least of all Bob."

"Good," Isabella said, taking a seat reluctantly. She poured a glass of beer and leaned back. "We don't need anyone else chasing it away, or getting killed. You cannot hunt something that has made a lifetime out of hiding by being loud or clumsy."

"We ain't clumsy," John Tyler said. It was the first time he'd spoken. "Me and Ned have hunted more in that swamp than anyone you're going to meet. We've gotten so close to deer, and bears, that we could have touched them. We didn't spook that thing. We caught it about to feed."

"You didn't kill it," Isabella said.

"No, we didn't. It didn't kill us neither. You haven't seen it, so I'm goin' to excuse you bein' rude. That thing out there is no bear. ʻ It's the biggest damn thing I've ever seen outside a zoo. I think we hurt it, but we didn't know, then, what we was up against."

"I think there will be plenty of time for your story once we hear how this all started," Bullfinch cut in.

Isabella held John Tyler's stare for a long moment. He didn't lower his eyes, and eventually, she smiled, and nodded. Bullfinch turned to Mack.

"The floor is yours, my boy. Let's get this started."

It took a while, but eventually the story wound its way around the table until it ended up back with Mack.

"So," he said. "We know where it came from, to a point. We know how it got loose in the swamp. We even know, to a point, what to expect when we encounter it. What we don't know, yet, is how to track it down, or what we should do once we do."

"We kill it," Isabella said. "What other answer would there be? It has killed, and it will kill again…"

"It was hunting," Ned said quietly. "I'd have kind of expected you to *get* that."

There was a moment of tense silence.

"No one wants it to kill again," Bullfinch cut in. "And certainly we don't want to lose any of our party. Still, this is a rather unique situation, even from our perspective, Isabella. This is not our… usual challenge. This creature is very natural, and it's been living in basic peace in the swamp for many years. While it has killed, the circumstances behind that killing aren't clear. I'm not suggesting we could leave it out there, but as a man of science, among other pursuits, I would be remiss if I didn't say that I hope we'll find a way to interact with it. The creature represents a single link between millions of years…"

"About a hundred and twelve million, give or take," Al Seidel cut in. "Sarcosuchus—they call it the "Super" Croc—lived in the Cretaceous Period. Fasolasuchus, which I think our friend actually is, was around even earlier. Sarcosuchus was the biggest damned crocodile that ever lived. They've found remains up to forty feet, but it's estimated they could have been considerably larger—they never stop growing. The longer that thing lives, the bigger it will get. That's a rarity. Most of your prehistoric creatures had a growth cycle, but these are a lot like modern crocs, just a heck of a lot bigger.

"It's also probably very territorial. They wouldn't have traveled around looking for food. They'd have a pool, or a pile of roots they stay under. They're opportunity feeders. Considering that there's only one, and the swamp is full of deer, bear, and all kinds of other game, it's not that surprising it was able to remain out of sight. If something got too close, it wouldn't hesitate, but it's not a predator, per se."

"So what in hell brought it out?" John Tyler asked, cutting in. "If it's been in there all this time, why now?"

"That's part of what we need to figure out," Mack said. "In fact, my guess is that once we figure that out, finding it won't be as hard. I have aerial maps of the entire swamp—all the surrounding areas. The shots are recent, and I'm hoping that if we all, particularly those of you familiar with the area, give them a look, we'll be able to narrow down something that has changed. Whatever caused all of this, it's new, so the first focus has to be on the area, and what has changed."

"Let's get to it then," Jasper said. He let out a huge burp, and the room grew silent. When he felt them all starting at him, he scowled. "What?"

Mack spread a pile of large, blown-up photos on the table. Cletus grabbed them and slid them past Jasper to Ned, who spread them out like a fan. He and John Tyler stood, reaching down now and then to re-arrange the photos, sliding them into place so that they represented a large rendering of the entire preserve.

They walked back and forth slowly, and no one spoke. Then, almost as if they were a single person, they stopped.

"You see it?" John Tyler asked.

Ned nodded. "I do, and I'm not surprised. Damn."

"What?" Jasper asked, leaning closer. He nearly spilled his beer, and Cletus pulled him back, grabbing his shirt and tugging.

"This," Ned said, ignoring Jasper and pressing his finger to a spot on the outer ring of the Virginia side of the swamp. "I almost missed it, but..."

"It's the color," John Tyler continued. "The water there, it used to be mossy—dark green. I haven't been in there in a couple of years—chicken company bought the land to grow feed. Fields run right up against the swamp."

"What's different?" Cletus asked.

"That water is brown," Ned said. "Almost yellow. That creek runs straight on into the swamp. You cross enough bogs and pools, you can follow it all the way to Lake Drummond."

"Chemicals?" Bullfinch said.

Ned nodded. "That's my guess. Something they're usin' on that corn. Never cared much for farms where you couldn't meet an actual farmer... don't seem right."

"They brought in some jobs and money," Al cut in, "but they mostly brought in their own people to fill the positions. I wonder if that could be why? Maybe they don't want anyone noticing what's going on?"

"That's right up against a state park," Cletus said. "If something toxic is leaking into the swamp, we can stop it..."

"Too late for our big scaly friend," Bullfinch said. "Let's take a look at all the areas near that waterway. Maybe we can narrow down its nest—if that's what you call it."

"Finally," Isabella said. "Show me where it lives."

Bullfinch glanced at her. "It's not likely to be there," he said. "It's moved out. It should give us a good place to start, though."

"That thing is going to want to be as close to its comfort zone as possible," Al chimed in. "You might not find it where it's lived, but you'll find it as close as it can stand to be. I think it would be a good idea to get around to where that contaminated water is, and try to get some samples, do some testing on it."

"Better not let the chicken-folk see you," John Tyler growled. "As likely to shoot as ask questions, and they'll call in the law. A lot of money in chickens…"

They all glanced at him.

"Just saying." He said. "Those people are serious, and connected, and if they're dumping something into a state park, they aren't going to want anyone pointing that out."

"I think, all things considered," Cletus said, "that Bob and his boys might pull a few strings if it comes to that. At least when we go in, I'll let him know we're there. Never hurts to leave a trail."

"We're going to need a plan," Bullfinch said. "I suggest we break into teams. John Tyler and Ned, they know the area. They would be best suited to scout that waterway. Also, if they wind up running into trouble of any sort, I think they've proven they can handle themselves. We have the maps, and I believe with Cletus and Jasper, perhaps Al, we can make our way toward that same area from the North Carolina side. We're going to need to be better equipped than we were last time… we could carry inflatable boats, for instance. We'll need to keep moving, once we start. There's a point after which we aren't going to make it back out without spending the night…"

"You are crazier than a jackrabbit in a dog pen," Jasper said. "You have *got* to be kidding. Did you see anywhere out there to pitch your pup tent? You can't camp in there…"

"No one is camping," Isabella snapped, "we are hunting."

"Lady, you nearly got taken out by a snake in the daylight, what do you think happens if you step in a nest of copperheads in the dark?"

"Enough," Cletus said. He stood, feeling worn out. "We don't have a choice. We're going to have to get that thing out of there, dead or alive, and we're going to have to do it quick—tomorrow, I think. What we could really use is an edge, something that might lure it, or we have to get a better idea where it's going to be... That's one big swamp, and heading across it from one side to other in the hope of finding this Sarchowhatzitasaurs is *not* a good plan..."

"I have a couple of ideas," Samuel said, clearing his throat. "I'm not going to be a lot of good out in that swamp, but if you give me some time to work it out, I might be able to give you that edge. I want to look through what Mr. Seidel brought us on that creature, and I want to go over my thoughts with Beatrice... and Mack. If I'm right, we're going to need some technical expertise..."

"What are you thinking?" Bullfinch asked.

"Let me make sure I have something before I get into that," Samuel said. "It's getting late, and there's not a lot of time if you are planning on doing this tomorrow."

"He's right about that," John Tyler said. "I'm ready for bed, assuming I can sleep knowing what might be just on the other side of the trees. We can be up and on our way to Virginia before dawn."

"We'll meet just after daybreak," Cletus said. "Jasper and I can get back over to the bed and breakfast. Geoffrey, if you folks have a line of credit anywhere nearby, I can come up with the equipment we need. I know some folks used to serve with the U. S. Coast Guard, and a couple of others who work out at Blackwater... Inflatables and equipment for this sort of trip are available...at a price."

"You're covered, my boy," Bullfinch said. "I believe we have the weapons we need as well.

Isabella tossed her head impatiently. It was obvious she thought they should all climb in the truck, take the boat back to the swamp, and hunt until it was over, but even Jasper had made a point. This was no ordinary hunt, and as civilized as the outskirts might seem, The Great Dismal Swamp was no simple battleground.

"Let's get to it then," Cletus said. "You folks see if you can find something that will help, I'm gonna see if I can find my bed. Jasper, you can have the couch if we can find it…"

They all rose, spending a moment shaking hands, and gathering what they'd brought.

Mack went straight to Samuel, who was already deep in conversation with Beatrice. Tiki was looking bright-eyed, if a bit disheveled. Mack held the cage as still as possible."

"What have you got?"

"I'm not sure, but I'm going to need some recording equipment, and then, if I'm right, something portable that can play that recording. Loud."

Mack frowned. "I can handle the recording, and I can get the equipment here to play it back…but what?"

"Just bring the bird and let's get back to our rooms," Beatrice said. She grinned. "We all have work to do."

As if on cue, Tiki started shuffling back and forth on his perch, his signature song bursting forth loud and shrill, his head dipping as if in honor of his lost love Gypsy…"

"I really REALLY hope you don't do that when the lights are out," Mack said.

Samuel and Beatrice laughed.

19

The road leading around the perimeter of the swamp ended at a fence, double-wrapped in shiny steel chain and padlocked. Ned pulled up to that gate and stopped, engine idling, as he and John Tyler considered their options.

"I could cut that," John Tyler said. "Might be able to wrap it back like it was still locked after. Wouldn't stand to a close inspection."

Ned nodded.

To the right, fields stretched out as far as they could see. A line of trees cut through the center of those fields, about two acres away, and beyond that, they both knew, were more fields. All of it was lined in rows of hip-high corn, waving in the breeze. To the left of the road was a ditch, probably four feet deep and muddy at the bottom, and beyond that, the swamp began. It wasn't a gradual thing. The edge of the state preserve was a snarl of trees and brush, thick and barely controlled. It was obvious that whoever had cleared the field had been forced to cut it right up to that edge, clear the ground, and that the fight continued to contain the green, growing mass beyond the ditch.

"We could just park—not here, but close—and go in on foot," Ned said. That fence can't go in very far—wouldn't be legal."

"Waterway is still about a mile up the road," John Tyler said. "Don't mind the walk, but if we do it in there," he nodded at the swamp, "it's gonna take some time. Not sure we have it..."

They both stared out across the fields. No one was in sight, but that didn't mean they weren't being watched. Chances were there were cameras. Maybe even a drone. The men who farmed those fields weren't like other farmers—at least not other farmers the two were familiar with. They wore matching blue jumpsuits. They drove equipment that shone and glistened in the sunlight. They watered the land meticulously with state-of-the-art hydration systems. They did not tolerate trespassing.

"How about we have it both ways," Ned said at last. "We'll hide the truck best we can, and then hoof it back here on foot. We can take the road, and if we see sign of anyone, or it feels like we're bein' watched, we'll head into the swamp. Closer we get before we have to do that, the sooner we'll get to that waterway."

J.T. nodded. "Sounds right."

Ned backed up, dipped the rear of the truck slightly into the ditch, and turned, heading back down the dirt road the way they'd come in. All sides of the field were lined with tall trees, and the land just beyond the fence belonged to a family the two knew well. The White's had been farming that stretch since Ned and J. T. were boys. It was them that sold the land to the chicken farmers in the first place, and there was no love lost across those borders.

Not far down the first row of trees was a turn-off. They'd parked there before when hunting, and knew that they could do so now without drawing undue attention. Ned killed the engine, and they climbed out, grabbing their gear from the back of the truck.

Without further conversation, they slipped on light packs, grabbed ammo and guns, and started back up the road toward the swamp, the gate, and the land beyond. As they rounded the corner, there was still no one in sight. Ned gripped the top of the gate and swung up and over. J. T. handed him their guns, and followed suit. A moment later they were headed down the road paralleling the swamp at a trot.

"Len, we've got a problem," Steve Hislop said. He was staring at a bank of black-and-white security monitors on the bench in front of him. His hand was on the intercom that connected him to his security team.

"What is it?" a terse voice replied. "We're busy out here."

"Whatever it is, it's going to have to wait," Steve said. "We've got visitors, and they're headed straight in to the south fields by the swamp. Another half-mile…"

"Got it."

Steve pulled his hand off the intercom and rose, a frown painted across his normally cheerful features. The south border was a problem. The corn fields were carefully maintained by a blend of chemicals, fertilizers, and pesticides. In proper quantities, they were legal and safe, but the company demanded a certain level of performance, and they'd been pushing the boundaries of legal and safe for months, trying to squeeze every last drop of yield from their crop.

The result of this was an overflow they hadn't prepared for. They had an agreement with a local disposal company, but there were limits. If they had processed all of their waste through proper channels, what they'd done to their crops and their fields would become obvious. Someone would notice and they'd be shut down, and that was something Steve Hislop couldn't allow.

"The chickens need feeding," he was fond of saying, "and I am the man to feed them."

That was well and good, as long as they managed to siphon off the extra waste and make it disappear. If no one noticed, he thought by the next year he could cut back on the chemicals, and the fertilizer. They only had to make it through this first year. So they compromised.

The irrigation system drained into several ditches, angling toward the dismal swamp. When only water flowed, it was considered a good thing—even a trace amount of fertilizer was allowable. It helped the vegetation and growth. There were (in theory) inspectors to maintain levels and to analyze the drainage, but inspectors, like most people, could be bought, and chickens were big business—old money. They were channeling all of their waste down a single ditch, hoping to push it far enough into the swamp, fast enough, that it would be swallowed. That ditch was in the south fields, and trouble was headed straight for it. He hoped Len could get down there quick enough and he hoped they could keep things under control. Len McMullan was a hard worker, meticulous and thorough, but he had a temper—and there was a lot at stake.

Ned heard the truck motors long before anyone came into sight.

"We're gonna have to hit the swamp," he said. "And quick."

John Tyler didn't hesitate. He dropped down into the ditch and started up the other side, pushing brush out of his way and ducking under low-hanging branches. Ned followed on his heels. The two disappeared into the underbrush and kept moving straight in. At first the ground was dry, and they made good progress, but after about twenty feet, it started getting muddy and soft. Pockets of water obscured by vines and cypress gripped at their boots. They ignored it and kept moving. When they were completely cut off from view, they stopped.

They could hear the engines of at least two trucks out in the fields, winding down as the vehicles neared and slowed.

"Damn," Ned said softly.

John Tyler turned and studied the terrain paralleling the field.

"We wait, or we move," he said. "They might come in after us. If they do, we'll be better served moving on as fast as we can. They might just sit out there and wait to see if we come back out…"

"Does us no good to stay here," Ned said. "We need to get to that waterway. Looks like we'll have to hit it a ways in and work our way back to the mouth, unless we find what we're looking for before that."

"Odds are, if it's pushed that thing out of its nest, we won't have to be too close to the chicken fields to find it," JT said. "Could have spread in pretty deep. Looks like we'll be followin' it in. I don't know about you, but I don't feel much like explainin' myself to whoever's in those trucks."

"They showed up pretty fast," Ned said. "Sort of like they were expecting someone, or had somethin' to hide."

"Sorta like…" JT said.

They turned then and started off through the swamp. They didn't make much sound, despite the rough going. They never did. Pretty soon, the sound of the truck's engines had faded, and all they had to concentrate on was footing and snakes.

Len McMullan sat in the cab of his truck and stared at the swamp. There was no one in sight, but he knew they were there. Whoever it was, they were quick, and they had heard the trucks coming. Hunters might have run, but it wasn't hunting season. He was trying to figure a reason for someone to be wandering around in the swamp, and he could only think of one. It might be government inspectors, but his money was on environmentalists, do-gooders bent on checking the run-off into the swamp. He'd known it was coming. There was too much life in that marshy wasteland for any sort of major change to go unnoticed, but he'd hoped it would take longer.

If they made it through this season, they could tone it down, reel it all in and do some damage control. They just needed a couple more months to meet quota. Now that was being threatened.

"What do we do?" his partner, Chuck Gainey, asked. "You want to go into the swamp after them?"

Gainey was a short, stout man with close-cropped hair and broad shoulders. Len knew the guy would dive into that murky water with him if he asked, but he didn't think it was going to help.

"The only thing they could be after that would matter to us is that tributary," he said. "We'll drive down there and, if we have to chase them, we'll go in from the mouth. If they're in there and headed that way, they'll have to stop. They might cross it, but it isn't going to be easy. It's our best chance of catching up."

Gainey nodded.

Len turned and waved the second truck off. No sense all of them sitting around when there was work to do. Then he pulled back into the road and started driving along the dirt track at the edge of the field. He didn't race—whoever they were following was on foot, and it was probably best not to give the impression that they were in a hurry. The less urgency they showed, the better. He drove at a pace that might indicate a routine patrol—not that patrolling corn fields could be considered in any way routine.

It only took about ten minutes to drive down to the irrigation ditch currently dumping into the swamp. There were pipes—if they heard of an inspection, and needed a fast cover-up, they could divert the flow along toward tanks in the distance. Len briefly considered ordering the pipes connected now, just until they found out what was going on, but he knew they couldn't afford to exceed their projected waste output by much without repercussions. It was one thing to fool a single inspector who wasn't looking for anything in particular, but quite another to stand up to a rigorous investigation.

Better to track the problem to its source, and, if possible end trouble before it began. Odds were it was just hunters or fishermen. Even if his initial suspicion was correct, and it was tree-huggers looking for "dirt" on them, problems like that could usually be stopped in their tracks by a well-drafted check. There was big money in chickens—something he'd never have expected to be important to him. He'd started in the Army, and ended up farming corn for a chicken empire. Now this.

"We'll park down by the ditch," he said. "First we watch for a while, see if anyone comes out. We don't see anyone, I'll call Hislop, and we'll grab the longboat. Couldn't hurt to take a short float in and see what's so interesting."

Gainey nodded, and Len parked in silence. The water running in a dark line in front of them had a green, almost yellowish tinge. The surface looked greasy. It slid off into the swamp like a rolling serpent, disappearing into shadow.

20

When they arrived at the river, it was with a much larger and more diverse group than on their previous attempt. Cletus and Jasper rode in Cletus' truck. Bullfinch, Isabella and Mack brought Samuel and Beatrice with them in the SUV, and as they were getting ready to drop the boat into the water, Al Seidel showed up on his odd, three-wheeled bike, a pack slung over his shoulder and a shotgun in a holster on the side of the bike, like he was some sort of modern-day cowboy.

Tiki Kowalski was not with them. They'd convinced Jasper's Pap to watch him, figuring the two of them could drive one another crazy and watch *Judge Judy* on TV. The bird had been a little disgruntled, being trundled off to yet another strange place, but he'd settled in soon enough when Pap brought out his bag of sunflower seeds.

The equipment was different this time, as well. The packs were larger, stuffed and tied up with a lot more than they'd carried in the first time, including two that held compressed inflatable rafts. They'd chosen an entry point farther in along the river where aerial reconnaissance had shown a nearly dry, solid path through the middle of the swamp.

Mack pulled several sealed cases out of the back of the SUV and carried them to the boat.

"You ain't gonna be able to cart all of that in there," Jasper said, watching, but not offering to help. "Ground is like soup in some places. A load like that'll sink you to your knees."

Mack grinned at him.

"This stuff isn't going in with us," he said. "It's going to have to be set up on the riverbank, maybe in the boat. Someone's going to have to be there to operate it."

Jasper scowled at the boxes.

"What is it?" he said.

"I'll explain when we get there," Mack said. "It may not work, but it's something Samuel, Beatrice and I came up with to help draw the creature out. If Samuel and Beatrice are right, this could be the key to our getting a decent shot at it."

"They goin' to be your operators?" Jasper said.

"Not sure," Mack said. He turned to Samuel and raised an eyebrow.

"Not a chance," Samuel said. "We've been waiting longer than any of you to see this—thought our chance had passed. Like I said last night, I'm not likely to be much good fighting or hunting in a swamp, but I need to *see* it after all this time. You'd have to tie me to the boat."

"Might be in the market for an operator, then," Mack said. "You interested?"

Jasper went back to the truck, grabbed his cooler, turned, and saluted. "If it means *not* traipsin' through that swamp and chasin' double-d-goddam dinosaurs, I'm your man."

They all laughed, but then they settled down and finished loading the boat. It was a large craft, but there was a lot of equipment, and there were a lot more people than there'd been the first time. By the time they were on board, they were sitting a little low in the water. Isabella turned, frowned at Jasper and his beer cooler, then started the engine and pulled out into the center channel of the river, pointing the nose into the swamp's interior.

There was little conversation as they left the trucks and civilization behind. It was slightly cloudy, but the sun was peeking through the trees, sending golden ripples over the water in their wake. The swamp was alive with sound. Birds sang, and here and there they spotted movement among the trees, deer and smaller animals. Very different from their last visit, when everything had been silent.

Mack kept his eye on a small GPS panel. When they had reached the entry point, he called out to Isabella, who turned and ran the nose of the boat gently up onto the shore. Cletus jumped down and tied them off, while the others grabbed packs, weapons, and equipment and joined him on the bank.

Bullfinch pulled out a radio, flicked it on, and clicked the microphone three short bursts. A moment later, John Tyler's voice crackled through the speaker, breaking up slightly, but clear enough to understand.

"We're following the water in," John Tyler said. "We have company—not sure if they are going to follow. They don't seem happy we're here. I can see why, too. Water's like some kind of yellow-green sludge."

"Try not to make too much contact," Bullfinch said. "There's no telling what it is. We'll need a sample."

"Already collected," John Tyler said. "It's clearing up a little, but it's slow going. There's not a lot of dry land here."

"Don't go in too far," Bullfinch said. "If our friend is nearby, you might not be able to maneuver quickly enough."

"Roger that," John Tyler said, "but we may not have a choice. If they stay out there, or come in after us, we're going to have to keep moving."

"We'll be starting in soon," Bullfinch said. "We're going to try and call it to us. No way, of course, to know if it will work."

"I've been thinking about that," Al said. "I'm pretty sure it will. That thing has been out there for a long time, and it's been alone. If there is even a scrap of genetic memory mapped into its tiny brain—did I mention they're not very bright?—it will come. It won't be able to resist. Sarcosuchus and Fasolasuchus are both believed by some experts to have mated for life…"

"Not sure whether I'm excited by that news, or sorry to hear it," Cletus said. "I've seen what that thing can do—not firsthand, but close enough. I hope we're ready for it. Particularly if its hormones are raging."

"I do not know about *we*," Isabella said. "But *I* am ready. This has already gone on too long."

"You aren't big on patience, are you?" Samuel asked. "Just what *is* your plan?"

"We kill it," Isabella said simply. "You can do whatever you like with what is left, but when I find it—and I will find it—only one of us will walk away."

"They don't really walk," Beatrice cut in. "More of a glide, unless it's in the water."

Isabella glared at her.

Samuel turned to Bullfinch.

"There is no chance we could tranquilize it, airlift it out some way?"

It was clear that Bullfinch was torn, but after a moment he shook his head.

"It's too risky, I'm afraid. It's big, and it's a killer. We have no way to gauge how much tranquilizer would be required to keep it down, and if we tried to pull it out of here by air, alive, we'd draw a crowd we don't want. I'm afraid there's really only one option."

Samuel looked away, staring out over the swamp. Beatrice walked up and put an arm around him.

"We'll get to see it," she said. "Samuel, it's more than we dreamed of. We'll get to study it. We might even get to try again…"

They all turned and stared at her then.

"What?" she said, a little defiantly. "Tell me you believe that no one else will do it? Wherever it is you plan to whisk it off to, no one will study it? No one will want to see—to know?"

"I can't say for certain," Bullfinch said. "But I promise you, when that study takes place, you will be part of it."

"Christ," Jasper said. "Those two idjits is the ones that set the damned thing loose in the first place. You ain't gonna let them grow *another* one?"

Beatrice turned quickly, and Cletus stepped in front of his friend before it got any worse.

"I think," he said, "we have enough on our plates trying to find and stop this thing without worrying over how we're gonna divvy it up. Odds are pretty damn good that if we're not careful there won't be as many opinions to sift through before the day is out. Besides, it was an oak tree and Hurricane Callie that let the thing loose, and Mother Nature who let it live. You can't really blame that on Samuel or Beatrice."

"Am I the only one," Seidel said, "who thought to bring a camera? We may not bring it back, but if I get a chance, we'll have video."

"That'll light up the double-d-goddam YouTube," Jasper said. "She kicks its ass," he nodded at Isabella, "make sure you catch that. We'll be able to sell the movie rights to the SyFy channel…"

As the others checked and donned the last of their gear, Al stepped over to where Mack was working with an electronic panel. He'd run heavy-duty wires to what appeared to be a small PA speaker. The whole thing seemed to be an amplifier of some sort. On the front were several USB ports, and a thumb drive protruded from one.

"That camera," Al said. "I have more than one. I wondered if you might take a look?"

Mack glanced up. Al opened a plastic case and lifted out what looked like some strange, Radio Shack toy. It was square, with four fans—or propellers. From the bottom of the thing, a small camera was aimed down from a bracket.

"Quadcopter?" Mack said. He grinned.

Al nodded. "I've flown it a few times, but it's going to get a little tricky in there. It can be programmed…"

Mack's grin widened. He flipped a couple of switches and the lights on his panel came to life. He turned to Jasper.

"Not much harder than a CB radio," he said. "Give us about five minutes to get started in, then flip this switch," he touched a button, but didn't press it. "That will start the audio. At first, run it up to about five. If it doesn't seem to be working, I'll give you a call on the radio in the boat. Keep it live. We can crank all the way to ten if we need to—that's two hundred watts. Out here the sound should travel a long way."

"But … what in hell *is* it?" Jasper asked.

"You'll see," Mack said. "Let's just say we're going to see how deep DNA memory goes."

Jasper scratched his head and shrugged. He glanced at his

cooler and grinned. "Flip the switch, turn the knob. I can do that. Hell, I do it on the damn TV every day."

"Knew I could count on you," Mack said. "And here, in case you get bored…"

He pushed a button on the boat's control panel and a tablet PC slid into view. Mack booted it up and began typing so fast that Al and Jasper could only stare.

"Al, that thing's Bluetooth or Wi-Fi?"

"Wi-Fi," Al said. "Bluetooth doesn't have enough range."

Mack nodded and kept typing. "Turn it on," he said. "Look for a Wi-Fi network named DINO—pass key supercroc."

Al did as asked.

"Got it," he said. "Signal is strong."

Mack nodded. "Turn on the camera."

Al did. Mack grunted once, typed a few more commands, and stepped back. On the screen they had a really clear image of Al's shoes.

"When we get out there, we can get it in the air," Mack said. "We can control it from your phone, or mine, but from here we can record the feed. We get anything worthwhile, Jasper will see, and if you see anything before we do, you can let us know."

Jasper shook his head and started chuckling.

"I'm puttin' this on my damn resume," he said. "Audio engineer and aerial photographer."

"Don't forget to send it to *National Geographic*," Al said. "If we get anything good, this could be important."

"Whatever," Jasper said. He turned to Mack.

"This thing get ESPN?"

Mack glared at him, and Jasper backed off, hands in the air. "Just kiddin'. I don't want anyone gettin' hurt, least of all Cletus. That boy still owes me a twelve pack."

Jasper leaned back in one of the comfortable seats on the boat. He didn't reach for his cooler until they were out of sight. The last thing he saw was Cletus, turning at the edge of the underbrush and waving. His friend smiled, but it was thin and forced. A moment before, staying behind on the boat had seemed like a safe bet. Now Jasper found himself glancing around for his shotgun, and wishing he'd brought in his own boat and the .50 caliber.

He popped the top on a beer and leaned over Mack's console. He flipped the switch as instructed and turned the knob up slowly. As he did so, the speaker emitted a loud, whistling chirp. He continued to turn the volume up until he reached five, then he sat back and took a long drink. He had heard the sound that was blasting from the speaker before, back at the Cotton Gin. It was the bird, that damned Tiki. The whistle was a pattern, repeated over and over. He frowned.

"Christ," he said. "I got to listen to this until they get back?"

The whistle rolled out and away into the swamp. Jasper shook his head and glanced at the tablet screen. Nothing yet. He sipped his beer and waited as the loud, eerie call rang out.

"What did they say they called that?" he muttered? "Chirpin' the bird?"

Big damn bird to be chirpin', he thought. *Hope to hell it doesn't piss the thing off.*

21

The recorded voice of Tiki Kowalski chirping followed them in, rising in volume until it evened out and blended with the sounds of the swamp. As they moved deeper in, the group slid into a formation. No one directed it, it just seemed to happen. Isabella was up front, and Cletus stayed close beside her. He was the one with the most experience in the swamp. Behind them, Bullfinch plowed along steadily, with Samuel and Beatrice flanking him, keeping a close eye on the brush to either side.

In the rear, Al and Mack whispered quietly. Al carried his quadcopter in one hand. Mack was fiddling with his phone. Even using his thumbs and on the small screen, his typing speed was almost superhuman. He flipped from application to application, checking the maps, his GPS, and revising the program he'd been coding to control the copter.

"Once it's in the air," he said, not looking up, "it will maintain the course we set for it. I've programmed it to head back to the river when the battery starts getting low. It will transmit the entire time, so if anything comes along, we should be able to get some of it on video. I'm setting it to follow the same course we've set for ourselves."

"I'm not worried about the copter," Al said. "The video is what's important. I can replace the hardware, so you can just let it keep tracking us until it dies."

"Okay then," Mack said. He punched a bit more code into the phone. "It's set to follow us until the battery dies or it loses our signal. It will track on the course I set, but it will adjust according to GPS transmissions from this phone. Whatever we see, it will see. We just have to wait for the right moment to get it into the air. If we wait too long, we might not have the chance. If we do it too soon, it could die before anything useful can be recorded."

"I boosted the battery pack," Al said. "There was a kit, which cost extra, but I wanted it to be state of the art."

"What were you going to film?" Mack asked.

"No idea. When we get through this, remind me to show you the things I've collected. I have a lot of… stuff. Everything from Acheulean axes to telescopes, cannonballs from wrecked ships. If Jim gets back in time, I'll show you the Mammoth tusk."

"As in wooly?" Mack said, eyes widening.

"Ten foot long," Al said. "He's getting it out of Alaska—only reason he's not here."

Mack shook his head. "And I thought I had some strange things. My trailer back in Arizona is set up to record signals from space. Nothing too interesting so far, but a guy can always hope."

Al laughed, and Isabella turned, glaring at them both. After that, they all moved in relative silence. The air was thick and heavy, and all around them the swamp was alive with insects, birds, and other creatures. Once or twice they heard heavy splashing sounds, but after stopping and listening, they were not repeated.

The trail they'd mapped out was reasonably dry. They made good time, and the audio from back at the river helped to mask their movements, providing something different and strange. After half an hour, the sound grew in volume, and Mack smiled.

"Jasper is still awake," he said.

"He's probably figured out by now that he's sitting alone a few stones throws from where Max and Bill ran into our friend. He's sweating bullets by now."

"I just wish we could tell if it was working," Samuel said. "I'll tell you, I've heard enough of that bird already to last me five lifetimes. It's about to drive me crazy."

Mack smiled.

"I don't know, I kind of like it. Something about that sound keeps me alert…"

"When we get out of here," Beatrice said, "*if* we get out of here, he's yours. The bird, I mean."

"You mean that?" Mack said.

"Absolutely. He's been with us a long time, and honestly, we got him on a whim because of, well, you know. Now here we are. He led us full circle, but I'm with Sammy. That little guy twists my last nerve."

Suddenly, Isabella stopped. She held up a hand, and they fell in behind her and grew silent.

"What is it?" Bullfinch asked. His voice was so soft it blended with the breeze.

Isabella pointed. About a half-mile away, right on the track they'd set, a flock of birds had burst into the air. Something was moving. They stood very still, almost not breathing. After nearly five minutes had passed, a second group of birds took flight. It was closer.

"There's a water channel there," Mack said, checking his maps. "It's almost like a small river, just to our left."

"Whatever that is," Bullfinch said, "it's coming this way."

Isabella nodded. She glanced around. They stood in a small clearing. There was brush on all sides. To the left, only a few yards in, was a large murky pool that probably led on its far side into the stream Mack had mentioned. It was mostly dry in all other directions.

"Quickly," she said. "Spread out and ready your weapons. We need to try to lure it into this open space. We don't want it in the water, and we don't want it to know we're here. If we are lucky, I think we can keep the element of surprise."

"What makes you think we can surprise it?" Cletus asked.

She stared at him. "How many times, Mr. Diggs, do you believe something has hunted it, in all the years of its life?"

Cletus grinned.

"I see your point."

Mack turned to Al.

"We have to pick our moment," he said. "I don't think the copter will spook it, but we don't know enough about this thing to be certain. I think we wait until the last minute."

"Agreed," Al said, "but here's the thing. If there is any water between there and here, it's not going to be long. People see crocodiles as clumsy and slow, but moving in a straight line, they're damned fast. This one is big, and it's strong, and if it's really following that godawful caterwauling, it's going to be here quicker than you think."

"Okay then," Mack said. "Let's get that thing in the air."

Mack pulled out his phone and flipped it open. He dialed, then waited.

"Jasper?" he said.

"Yep… guess y'all are still alive."

"So far. Listen, we've got something big moving out here," Mack said. "We're about to put that copter live. Let me know you get the signal."

"You got it, boss," Jasper said.

Al held the small craft up level and flipped a switch to activate it. Mack tapped a couple of keys, and the four props began to whirr. Moments later it lifted off and rose straight up through the trees and brush. Mack made a few adjustments, bringing it just over head and beyond the low-hanging treetops.

"There she is," Jasper said. "Picture's clear, but mostly it's the tops of trees."

"Can you see us?" Mack asked.

"Yep. Hey Cletus!"

"Can't talk, Jaz," Cletus said. "Keep an eye out for us. Odds are you'll see it before we do."

"If it doesn't hear you first," Isabella snapped.

Cletus fell silent. Mack signed off quietly and they spread out. Cletus had his twelve-gauge, but it suddenly felt less adequate than any weapon he'd ever held. The others had a variety of guns. Mack moved into the shadows with Al, and a moment later, he whistled and let out a low laugh that got him another glare from Isabella.

"What is it, man?" Bullfinch said. "What in the *world* could be funny?"

"I don't know what it is," Mack said, "but if I were guessing, I'd say it's the first fifty-caliber pistol I've ever seen."

Al Siedel wasn't a tall man. He was broad-shouldered, but even so, the pistol in his hand looked like something out of a cartoon.

"Got a grenade, too," he said. "In case we need it."

At that, even Isabella let out a quick snort. She turned quickly to hide it, and they fell silent. After a moment the only sound was the occasional flight of birds, growing closer and closer, and the soft whirr of the quadcopter hovering overhead, broadcasting its images back to the river.

Jasper sat up straighter. The tablet screen flickered, went dark, and then came to life. He leaned forward and stared. After a moment the signal cleared and he saw what the camera saw—a wide-angle view of the swamp. He could make out water and trees, and in a clearing on one side of the screen, he saw one of their party. It was hard to tell who it was, but he thought it might be Cletus.

The small copter circled slowly, and as his mind accustomed itself to the view and arranged it to make sense, he was able to pin down the boundaries of the clearing and spot all of those who'd gone in—still safe. The circular flight pattern also gave him a view of a small perimeter around them. He wished he had control of the copter because as it circled, bits and pieces of the area came in and out of focus.

If they all started moving again, the copter would track them, but since they were stationary, it had gone into a holding pattern. Jasper watched carefully. He wanted to be able to see the water on the far side of their position, but he could only catch it once per pass.

He wished that Mack would talk to him, tell him what was going on, but the radio remained silent. Whatever had them spooked was too close. They weren't going to alert it by making any unnecessary sound or by moving.

As the copter swung slowly around for another loop, Jasper caught sight of something he hadn't seen before. It was hard to tell exactly what it was. In the water, there was a moving "V", but so big it nearly stretched the width of the waterway. It looked like some sort of very large log was shooting toward them, but not a log from any tree you'd find in the swamp. It was big around as a hippo, or some kind of small submarine, and it was moving very quickly.

"Holy crap," he said.

He reached for the radio. He hoped that on the other end it wouldn't let off a loud squawk, or start singing some double-d-goddam ring tone jingle. He thought of the Bat-phone on the old TV series and prayed it would just make a light blink. Then, as the thing started to rise slightly from the water, he realized it didn't matter if it sang the damned national anthem. He pushed the *Transmit* button.

"You hear me, you get ready," he said. "That thing is coming in fast, and it's as big as a truck. Jesus… it's huge."

He let his finger slip off of the button and kept his eyes on the screen. Maddeningly, as he did so, the copter circled on around, losing the image of the creature and making him question what he'd actually seen. Could it have been a big fish? A log? The only sound he'd picked up so far was the whirring of the blades, but as the camera swung out of range, he heard a crash, the splash of water, and then a roar so loud, so overpowering, that the microphone on the camera peaked and overloaded, and he pushed back and away from a screech of static.

"Holy hell!" he said. He slid back down onto the seat and watched, waiting. All he could see was the tops of trees, but off screen he heard screams and at least one gunshot. He thought he heard Cletus curse, and he shook his fist at the tablet.

"Get that damn thing, Cletus," he said. Then, as an afterthought, "damned freakin' dinosaur…"

22

Ned and John Tyler had followed the waterway about a mile into the swamp. If anyone was following, they were doing it quietly, but the going was getting rough. Vines clung to their legs, and twice they'd had to shift directions to avoid deeper water.

"Should be dry ahead," Ned said, "but it's a long way around that lake."

"I don't like the way that water smells," John Tyler said. "Some kind of chemical. And I ain't seen a snake since we came in. No turtles on the logs. Something is *seriously* wrong here."

"Just try to keep it on the outside of your boots," Ned said. "I've got plenty of samples…so we need to figure out what we're going to do. We go back, we might have company waiting. We move on ahead, we're likely to be stuck out here all night. You ready for that?"

"Not really." Swamp is one thing. I could find a place to pass the night—done it a thousand times—but that thing…"

"Yeah, I don't think it's coming back here, but it might," Ned said. Then he stopped and stood very still. "You hear that?"

"What?" John Tyler said. They stood very still, and the sound repeated. It was very weak, and very far away, but it sounded like some sort of whistle."

"A bird?" Ned said, shaking his head. "Damned big one if it is. What the hell?"

"I bet it's the others," John Tyler said. "Don't know why they think that'll do it, but I bet they're tryin' to lure the damn thing."

"We could follow the sound. If they are trying to draw that

monster, we might just flank it. If it doesn't just kill them all and turn back on us. There's another waterway that cuts straight over there on the map. We can follow that all the way to the river."

"Don't have much firepower."

"I got a surprise for you," Ned said. He grinned. "Didn't really feel like coming out here unprepared. I talked to that guy Al, fella on the bike? He hooked me up yesterday."

"With what?"

Ned reached into his pack, fumbled around a moment, and then pulled out a small, round object. At first John Tyler didn't see what it was. Then his eyes got wide.

"A damned grenade?" he said. "You came out here with a grenade in your backpack and didn't think, 'Ned, you should let John Tyler know about this... might come in handy knowin' it's there when them cotton-pickin' chicken pluckers turn us over to Sheriff Bob and they find it in your pocket... '"

Ned's grin got wider. "Nope, didn't even cross my mind. I was thinkin' that when you walk your dumb ass straight into a damned dinosaur's nest, I'd pull 'er out and save you. Then you'd owe me."

"Like hell," John Tyler said. Then he grinned. "Okay, we go in then. I don't really feel like backtracking through that goo. If there was any chance of my havin' kids someday, I think we just cut it in half walkin' through there."

"Thank the Lord for small favors," Ned said. He tucked the grenade into his jacket pocket, and the two set out. About twenty minutes later, as the whistling sound was growing loud enough to get irritating, they heard a gunshot. Ned glanced at John Tyler, and then the two began to run.

23

Everything happened at once. **Jasper's warning squawked into** Mack's earpiece and he tried to pass it on, but it was almost too late to be of value. There was a sliding, sloshing sound, and then the air seemed to shatter from the sound of a roar so loud, so over-powering it rattled teeth and echoed through the swamp. A huge shadow rose from the water directly in front of them. Cletus dove left, spinning and firing from the hip, managing to get two blasts from his shotgun before he hit and rolled.

Bullfinch grabbed Mack by the arm and pulled him behind a slightly thicker stand of trees. Then he separated himself and stood, calmly, like he was drawing down on a stand of quail. His back was straight, and he aimed carefully, firing shot after shot at the underside of the thing as it rose, and rose, towering over them and screaming again.

Al Seidel had wrapped his arms around a tree, using a branch as a brace. He fired the huge, .50-caliber pistol and Mack saw a chunk slip off the hide of the creature. It wasn't a serious wound, but it hurt the thing, and it kept it from crashing straight over into the middle of the clearing and crushing them.

"We're not hurting it," Mack said. "All we're doing is making it mad."

Isabella paid no attention to any of them. As they distracted the creature, blasting away at it with everything they had and forcing it to duck its head and protect its face, she ran. She left the clearing, sped along the edge of the water, then curled back.

Ahead of her, the thing had slipped back and dropped into the water. It still towered over her, but its head was down, concentrated on those attacking and it didn't see or hear her. She sped up, and just before she actually came up beside it, she leaped. In each hand she held what appeared to be a black staff. With a scream that nearly rivaled that of the creature, she landed on its neck, clamped down with her legs and drove the two staves into the sides of its head.

Two almost simultaneous explosions erupted at the points of impact. Despite her grip, the force of it drove her up and back. She flew past the almost impossible length of the creature's thrashing tail. She spun in the air and landed feet first in the water, then disappeared.

The creature reared in pain and anger. It screamed again and shook its head from side to side, thrashing its huge tail. Bullfinch, still standing calm and still as a stone, stepped forward and began firing again, trying to aim for its eyes, or to get a shot at anything below the spiny, scaled back and into the thing's chest. Cletus stepped up beside the older man, and added his shotgun's voice to the attack. Samuel and Beatrice had fallen back, as if stunned. Samuel lifted his shotgun and aimed, but didn't seem to remember what it was he should do with it.

Then Al, still gripping the trunk of the tree tightly for support, unloaded again with the huge, .50-caliber pistol. Each time he fired it, his arm whipped up and back and it threatened to knock him from his feet. The shots were hurting the creature, but despite all the damage, it was still moving, thrashing in pain and shock and anger. Isabella, who had climbed from the water, ran back to where the others waited. She seemed surprised that the creature hadn't gone down.

"What the hell were those things?" Cletus asked, reloading as quickly as he could.

"Bang Sticks," she said. "I have used them on crocodiles and sharks. These are the biggest we have."

"Not big enough," Cletus observed. "That thing is really pissed off now."

"Wait," she said. "The loads were dual—explosive and tranquilizer.

It should be enough to at least slow it down."

Cletus passed this along to Bullfinch and to Mack, who glanced over and saw Samuel and Beatrice pulled back from the group. Samuel still held the shotgun in trembling hands, but showed no sign of using it. Mack ran to them.

"Get back toward the river," he said. "We'll finish this."

Behind him, the .50-caliber pistol boomed and another round of shotgun blasts drove the creature into a new frenzy. It half-turned away from them, from the source of pain and danger, toppling like a great tree toward the water. It *was* looking sluggish, but despite all their firepower and the tranquilizers, it was still moving, turning away.

"We have to stop it!" Isabella screamed. She reached into her pack, pulled out two more of the bang sticks, and started after the retreating monster at a run.

"Isabella, wait!" Mack cried. He took off after her, unable to catch up, but moving quickly. Samuel and Beatrice slipped back into the trees without a word or an apology.

"What the hell do we do now?" Cletus said, turning to Bullfinch and Al. "I can't run like that."

"There is no force in nature that could stop Isabella now that the fight has begun," Bullfinch said. "We'll follow as quickly as we can."

He started off at a slow trot. Cletus shrugged, and Al grinned. They followed Bullfinch into the swamp, chasing the crashing of the great beast's retreat and the cries of their companions.

Isabella caught up with the lumbering beast after less than 100 yards. It wasn't moving as quickly as it had before, and its progress was erratic. Once it rolled halfway over on one side, as though dazed. Mack was just starting to gain on her when, without hesitation, she leaped again, landing with both feet on the thing's broad, half-submerged back and bracing herself with her knuckles, the bang sticks gripped tightly. She balanced for a moment, as if surfing, and then took off again, actually running up the thing's spine toward its head.

"The eyes!" Mack called after her. "Go for the eyes!"

If she heard him, she made no move to acknowledge it. Her balance was uncanny, as the thing rolled and glided down the stream of murky water. Mack cursed and tripped along the bank, trying to keep up, but even drugged and hurt, the big croc was fast.

Isabella moved steadily forward. Low-hanging braches and vines threatened to dislodge her, but each time, as if by some sixth sense, she ducked or turned, avoiding the obstacle and moving forward once more.

Mack pushed through the brush, fighting to keep her in sight. Either her steps were incredibly light, or the thing was just too far gone to care about an annoying weight on its back. It kept moving forward unsteadily.

Isabella lunged at its head. She raised the bang sticks, but as if anticipating what was to come, the beast rolled. She flailed for a moment, caught her balance, and drove the weapons down, but her aim was spoiled. Like the first time, she made contact with the tough hide on either side of the massive neck. This time she didn't have the grip with her legs to help support her, so the impact drove her back immediately. She rolled with it, but the pain woke the creature, and it reared again. She tumbled head over heels, managing a single somersault before reaching the tail. At that moment, it thrashed. Isabella tried to grip the thick hide but the tail moved too fast—too hard. With a cry she launched into the air, flying up and over the first line of trees, almost directly above Mack's head. She passed the hovering quadcopter in flight, and Mack briefly wondered just what Jasper would see on the far end.

He stopped, uncertain what to do. If he went to help her and she was okay, but the creature escaped, she might just kill him. If he ignored her, she might be hurt—even dying. Before he could decide, a shout sounded up ahead of the creature. Then another. Someone was out there, and the thing was headed straight to them.

The river in front of them exploded as Ned and John Tyler broke through a stand of trees. They instinctively split, John Tyler dove to the right and Ned spun to the left. He didn't have the same luck as his partner, though. His foot caught in a vine, and he tumbled over sideways, crying out and cursing as he went.

In the water, the creature caught the motion, and then the sound. It was almost fully awake again, after Isabella's second pair of bang sticks had dug into its hide, and having nothing else to focus on, it turned toward Ned.

Ned didn't spend any time calculating his odds of escape. He reached into his pocket, pulled out the grenade and pulled the pin. He kept his thumb tight on the grip. He had one shot—one in a million—to get this thing. If the grenade went off by its head, it might stun the creature, but it wasn't going to take it down. The hide was too thick… only one thing would do it, and if it was the only way to help keep John Tyler and the others safe, Ned was willing to step up and do it.

The monster let out another hideous roar, the sound so loud it rippled through Ned's hair, and the thing's breath so thick and foul it choked him. He closed his eyes, just for a second, and when he opened them he saw it looming over him, jaws wide. Then it struck. With a scream of defiance, Ned whipped his arm up and lobbed a perfect strike. The grenade entered the creature's mouth and disappeared inside. It hardly noticed. Ned rolled then, scrambling to his feet and putting every ounce of strength remaining to him into diving free.

There was another bang behind him, but he ignored it. Too small to be the grenade. Then he heard John Tyler cursing and turned back. His friend stood directly below the rearing creature, furiously pumping his shotgun and firing into the thing's throat.

"Damn it, JT!" He shouted. "Get out of there!"

John Tyler made no move to comply, and Ned headed back toward the water, waving his arms wildly. "Get out of there you damn fool, the grenade is going to…"

The explosion cut him off cold. The sound was so overwhelming, and so close, that, rather than seeming loud, after the first moment it became an absence of sound—a void. Ned crashed forward toward the water, but he was driven back by a hard splatter of scales and bone and gore. It knocked him from his feet and he lay, stunned, in the soft peat moss, staring up through the cypress trees into the sky.

24

The explosion caught all of them off guard. Mack, who'd been hesitating, was close enough to be thrown from his feet. He didn't see Isabella, just crawling from the murky water to the relative dry ground of the bank, or hear her cry out as the impact of the creature's fall, close on the compressed explosion that had removed the top of its head and ripped a slash down the center of its back, toppled her back into the water.

Bullfinch managed to grip a tree and remain standing for the spectacle, as did Al. Over their heads, blindly following the signal from Mack's cell phone, the quadcopter whirred and circled.

From his vantage, Bullfinch had seen Isabella fall back into the water. He ran to the bank, saw her struggling back up from the mud again, and leaned down to offer her a hand. He hauled her up and out and she stood, dripping wet, covered in mud, her eyes blazing.

"What…just happened?" she asked. "I hit that thing again—and it threw me. Next thing I know someone is shouting, and then…"

"Grenade," Al said, stepping up beside them. "I have one with me, but I gave one to that guy Ned last night. I think maybe the cavalry arrived just about when we needed them."

Isabella looked as if she was about to argue the point, but instead, turned silently and stalked off along the bank toward where Mack was climbing to his feet. They found Ned standing on the bank, staring out over the water. The beast's body had bottomed out near the bank. It rose from the water like a small island. Bloody bits of flesh and bone were everywhere. The water had settled and was lapping against the thing's side.

"Where's John Tyler?" Mack asked.

Ned only pointed with his chin. His eyes were wide, and his jaw worked several times before he managed to get any sound out.

"He was in there with it," he said at last. "Tried to tell the damned fool about the grenade, but he was too busy trying to bust a hole in it with his shotgun to listen. That thing had me...would have bit me in two as sure as the sun shines, but JT stepped up and took after it."

"A brave man," Bullfinch said. He dropped a hand lightly onto Ned's shoulder. "Let's see if we can't find him, shall we?"

Ned came to life as if he'd been poked with a hot iron. He sloshed out into the water, heedless of the others reaching out to slow him down, and headed straight for what they could see of the creature's head. He used his arms to help propel him through the water and circled around. In moments he'd disappeared from sight completely on the far side of the slowly bobbing carcass.

"Now what?" Cletus said. "We can't just leave it here. How are we going to get something that big out of this place without attracting all the wrong kinds of attention? Hell, I don't even want to have to tell Sheriff Bob about it..."

They stood and stared. It was impossible to tell from the bank just how big it was. The head was the size of a speedboat, and the body stretched out behind it and under the water.

"It *is* a bit of a problem, isn't it?" Bullfinch said.

"I might know a guy..." Al Seidel said, cutting in. "He's done a lot of logistic work with the Coast Guard. Retired now, but he still 'dabbles' now and then. If anyone can figure out how to airlift a dinosaur out of the swamp, it's him. If I work with him, we can get it out of here for you. You'll have to take ownership pretty quickly though. Got nowhere to store that thing, and I doubt Homeland Security is going to want it in one of their hangars."

There was a sudden whoop from the water.

"Some help in here?" Ned shouted. "He's alive."

Mack shrugged off his pack and handed his phone to Bullfinch, then sloshed into the water and followed the sound of Ned's voice.

He found the man leaning down, holding John Tyler's head out of the water.

"Damn thing's foot is on his leg," Ned said. "I can't budge it."

Mack circled around, tested the weight, and frowned. The creature shifted slightly. The water was moving around them, flowing from the river in the distance in toward Lake Drummond. It wasn't moving quickly, but there was enough current that the huge body rocked against the shore in a sort of rhythmic undulation.

"Hold on," Mack said. "I have an idea."

He climbed up the opposite bank and disappeared into the trees. A moment later he returned. He carried a branch about the circumference of his arm. He dug the end of the pole into the mucky bottom of the river.

"Feel how it's rocking?" he asked.

Ned nodded.

"I'm going to count down from three," Mack said. "When it rocks up toward the bank, I'm going to lift on its leg with this pole. When I do that, I need you to pull him out of there. We'll have to be quick. If I can lift it, it won't be for long, and it will settle again quickly."

"Let's do it," Ned said.

Mack turned, pressed his shoulder to the pole, and began to count. The body rolled and he braced himself and shoved, using his legs and keeping his back as straight as possible. He'd spent long hours on surfboards, snowboards, rock climbing, distance running. The thrill of adrenaline coursing through his veins was the only other thing that could hold his attention beyond the data, and the continual flow of information and patterns. He was strong—a lot stronger than he looked. He pushed, and just a little, the monstrous form gave way.

"Now!" he shouted.

Ned pulled. John Tyler slipped free, dragging on the bottom and pulling gouts of slick mud along with him, but he was out. The creature dropped back into place, and Mack fell, landing butt first in the water, the makeshift lever flying off over his shoulder. Ned fell too, but managed to keep John Tyler's head above the water. A moment later, his friend started to sputter.

"Let's get him back to the others," Mack said. "Meanwhile, tell me what you found at that inlet. I have an idea what do with our overlarge friend here, but it may depend on what you have to report."

As they helped John Tyler up the far bank and handed him over to Cletus, Samuel and Beatrice re-appeared through the brush. They stared wide-eyed at the dead beast.

"You two have some medical background, yes?" Isabella said, glaring. "That man needs assistance."

Beatrice snapped out of it first. She hurried to Ned's side and helped him lay John Tyler back on the ground. Samuel joined her, and in their favor, the two worked quickly and efficiently, examining the leg that had been trapped for broken bones and treating for shock. Meanwhile, Ned filled Mack in on what they'd found at the chicken-feed farm.

Mack nodded, then called Al over. "If you can get that friend of yours in here with something big enough to move this, I think I know where we should take it. I'm going to need to make some calls, and we're going to have to pay a visit to that farm."

"We get John Tyler settled," Ned said, "I'll go with you. Got to pick up the truck anyway."

Something overhead whirred erratically, and they all glanced up. The quadcopter, its battery dying, still circled. Its motions had become erratic, and it was losing altitude. Then, very suddenly, the rotors locked and it plummeted.

Without warning, Isabella launched after it. Just as it was about to strike the water, she leaned out and plucked it from the air. Then, as if nothing out of the ordinary had happened, she walked back and tossed it to Al, who caught it clumsily.

"Your toy almost got wet," she said.

They all stared at her, and then, very suddenly, started laughing. It rose in just seconds to nearly hysterical levels as the stress they'd built up and held released in a rush. Isabella stared at them, one, then the other, and turned, walking back through the trees toward the river.

A few moments later, after determining, with help from Cletus and Ned, that John Tyler could walk, the others followed. Beatrice stopped by the water, just for a moment, and stared down at the giant, lifeless hulk. Then, with a quick shake of her head, she hurried after the others. Moments later nothing remained but the huge body rolling gently in the current. Slowly, the sounds of other wildlife returned.

25

The CH-47 Chinook hovered over the swamp like a huge, shadowy bird. The soft *thwup!* of the props sent spray flying off the surface of the streams and ponds and laid the grass and brush flat. On the ground, men in fatigues moved quickly and efficiently, securing huge cargo nets and straps. They had rolled the giant carcass onto its side and worked it on to the nets, then pushed it back and used the natural buoyancy of the dead body to slide the nets under and around.

When all was secure, they stepped back, and the man leading the crew on the nets waved his flashlight in a slow arc. There was an answering flash from the helo, and it began, very slowly, to rise, lifting the body of the Fasolasuchus or Sarcosuchus, or whatever it was into the air, dripping muck and moss, dirty water and slightly rotted guts as it went. The ground crew pulled back.

A radio crackled, and the ground supervisor answered.

"Thanks, John, we've got it from here."

"Take it easy with that load. There was no way to get it properly balanced. It's going to be tricky."

"Careful isn't my thing," Al replied.

The helo rose slowly until its burden was well clear of the trees, and headed off toward the northwest corner of the swamp. John Siemens stood and watched it go, then shook his head and turned away.

"Let's get this gear packed and cleared out," he said. "We need to get it back and cleaned up before someone notices it's gone…"

Len McMullan heaved on a long, taut length of rope and secured it to a wooden stake pounded deep into the field. Others were performing the same task up and down the way. The framework was in place, and all that was left was for whatever the men in the long, slick black cars and SUVs were dropping into place to arrive so they could erect the tarpaulin covers and lash them into place. It was late, and he wanted to get home, get some food, have a beer and forget he'd ever seen corn, The Great Dismal Swamp, or that goo they'd been pumping into it.

He saw Gainey about half an acre away, working with another crew. Hislop was still back in the office, which was full of men in very black suits who didn't have a smile among them. They'd come in so fast the events were a blur. A line of official vehicles. Phone calls, trucks full of equipment, and no resistance whatsoever.

Not that it would have helped. Whoever these guys were, they had corporate's ear in a big way, and they had assumed control. Len was vague on the details, but the gist of it was that something big, important, and very hush hush was incoming. They would cover it up, look the other way until it was loaded and disappeared, and in exchange, the spill in the swamp would be cleaned up—and forgiven. There were conditions of course—it couldn't happen again—but all things considered, judging from the men in charge, it was a better deal than they deserved.

The sound of a helicopter approaching caught his attention. He glanced up, saw lights in the distance, and started working faster.

"Incoming," he shouted. "Get this thing ready to go. Whatever it is, it's almost here."

All along the field, men worked furiously, tightening the lines and readying themselves to pull the tarp up and over whatever it was they were expected to conceal. Len only spent a couple of seconds wondering about it, then he shrugged it off. Whatever it was, he was probably better off knowing as little as possible.

The helo approached slowly, and he saw that, whatever the cargo was, it was very large, and oddly shaped. It dangled, a huge shadowy form supported by cargo nets.

"Get the truck in here!" He called. "Get it in here now! That thing is coming in, and there'd better be something under it when it does!"

He heard a diesel crank, and slowly, directed by men along either side, a large tractor trailer was backed into place. It stopped dead center between the lines of ropes and men. What seemed only moments later, the helo began dropping, its cargo wavering slightly as it jockeyed for position.

Men with lighted cones waved it into position, and after a few adjustments, the wind whipping dirt and leaves up all around them and worrying at the tarpaulin that made up the gigantic tent they'd constructed, the cargo settled onto the trailer, slightly crooked. It was very long, and smelled like hell warmed over. Men climbed up the sides of the truck and released the hooks holding the nets, which fell down and draped over the sides of the trailer.

The helo lifted off and soared away to the south. Len and others down the line called out, and lines were pulled. The tarpaulin was pulled into place, blotting out all sight of the trailer, the truck, and whatever now rested on it. In only a few moments the work was complete, and the lines were tied off.

Chuck Gainey made his way down the field to where Len stood, staring at the tent.

"What in hell do you think *that* was?" he asked.

Len shook his head. "No idea. It smelled like something dead dragged out of the swamp, but it was big. Unless a circus lost an elephant recently, I haven't got a clue. I also don't care. If we hurry, we can get in to Coasters before they close."

Chuck stared at the tent a moment longer, and then nodded.

"Sounds about right. I'm gonna see if Hislop can get free. He might know something…"

"Don't want to know," Len said. "Whatever it is, it's important enough for Uncle Sam's goons, or whoever's goons, to come in here and wipe out something that was likely to put us all in jail. If we walk away from this free men who still have jobs, I'm calling it a win."

"Well," Gainey said, turning to glance at the huge tent a final time, "whatever it is, it stinks like a sewer…"

They walked up and down the line, checked with the others, and, once they were certain the job was complete, they climbed into their truck and headed back to the main office. The parking lot was filled with a row of dark, sleek SUVs. Every light in the building was lit.

"I don't think Hislop is getting out there anytime soon," Len said. "I say we head on to Coasters. He'll catch up if he can."

They backed up and drove slowly away, hitting the winding dirt road where Ned and John Tyler had arrived earlier that day. They passed right on by the farms, and out onto the freeway beyond. They did not look back.

26

"**W**here will they take it?" Beatrice asked.

They were gathered again at the same table in the back of the Cotton Gin. They'd taken time to clean up, for the most part. John Tyler had been taken to the hospital in Elizabeth City for observation, and Ned had stayed with him. Bullfinch had spent the last couple of hours coordinating a seemingly endless fleet of government vehicles, stern-faced agents, and others. Isabella ignored them all, her task complete. She had not smiled since they'd left the swamp, and she'd spoken very little.

Cletus and Jasper were nursing a half-full pitcher of beer. Mack had a laptop and several screens going at once at one corner of the table, and Al was with him. Among other things, they were editing what video they'd gotten.

Bullfinch turned to Beatrice.

"It's being taken to a research facility in Colorado," he said. "I've arranged accommodations for the two of you, and travel, if you'd like to be part of the team. It would mean a move, I'm afraid. It could take years to learn all that we can from the creature."

Beatrice nodded.

"Of course we'll go," Samuel said. "How could we not?"

"We will help with your things, and the move," Bullfinch said. "I think you'll find our resources are rather extensive."

Samuel chuckled. "I'd rate that as the understatement of a lifetime," he said. "I've never seen so many black suits, black cars, trucks, planes or so many people appear—and then disappear—without a trace."

"Our work isn't the sort of thing one parades in public," Bullfinch said. "We tend to keep as low a profile as is possible."

A sudden sound at the far end of the table silenced them all, and they turned. Perched in his cage, strutting back and forth and tilting his head, as if to hear better, Tiki Kowalski had begun his dance. It was a very determined effort, and showed no signs of quick abatement.

Beatrice walked down the table and laid a hand on Mack's shoulder.

"What do you think?" she asked. "I believe Mr. Kowalski has taken a liking to you."

"It's funny," Mack said. "I thought the sound would be distracting, but somehow it calms me..."

"Then it's settled," Beatrice said. "The only living member of the Crockatiel family will come to live with you. If my calculations on his age are correct, you've got another fifteen to twenty years of this."

Bullfinch winced.

"Don't worry," Mack said. "He'll be in the computer room with me, or in my room. I think it's about time I had a companion."

Tiki cocked his head and glared at Mack, then went back into his dance, unperturbed. They all laughed.

Al Seidel made a round of the table, shaking hands, and saying his farewells.

"I have to get out to Arizona," he said. "I'm meeting someone there. I think they found something pretty cool up in one of the canyons, but we won't know until we've started digging..."

"Good luck, then," Bullfinch said. "Try not to bring back anything living. I've had more than enough dinosaur hunting for one lifetime."

"Funny," Al said, "I've been hunting them all my life—the past—dinosaurs, early men, whatever I can find. It's fascinating stuff..."

"Indeed," Bullfinch said. "One day I hope to make it back this way and see the rest of that collection you told me about."

"You'll be welcome. If I'm not there when you call, my wife will tell you where to find me. We've got plenty of room."

"Is she a collector then?" Bullfinch asked.

"Sue?" Al chuckled. "She collected me. I think that might be enough for her…she tolerates the rest."

One by one, they gathered their things and headed out the door. Eventually, only Cletus, Jasper, Mack and Bullfinch remained. Isabella had gone out to see to the stowage of what remained of her gear.

"She's still mad she didn't kill it isn't she?" Cletus asked.

Mack grinned. "You nailed it. I think she's a little embarrassed she needed help."

"It was a *damn dinosaur!*" Jasper said. "She *needs* to cut herself some slack…"

"Yeah, well, that's not likely," Mack said. "She's not a 'slack-cutting' kind of girl. She'll get over it. I meant to thank you for the warning. You probably saved our lives."

"I sat in a damn boat," Jasper said. "Kinda wish I'd been there."

"Maybe this will help," Mack said. He pulled a wrapped package out of his pocket. "I already gave one to Al—they've authorized one for each of you. Just in case you need to remind yourselves it really happened. The two extras are for Ned and John Tyler, when you see them."

Jasper took the package and turned it over a couple of times, then unwrapped it carefully. Inside, wrapped in soft cloth, was the biggest tooth he had ever seen.

"Whoa," Cletus said. "Are you tellin' me *that* is what we almost got on the wrong end of?"

"These are only mid-sized," Mack said. "The really big ones would have crushed your skull."

"Thanks," Cletus muttered. "*That* will help me sleep better at night."

"At least it's gone," Jasper said.

"Yeah, probably no more of those out there," Mack said.

"Probably?"

He turned, picked up Tiki Kowalski's cage, and headed for the door.

"Now wait just a double-d-goddam minute," Jasper said, half rising to follow. "What do you mean *probably*?"

"Well," Mack said, "There were three viable samples in the broken cooler he came out of, and according to Eddie Dodd, the original is still alive, if injured, running around the jungles of Brazil…"

He winked at them, turned, and headed out to the parking lot. The door closed behind him with a *thunk!* Jasper dropped back into his seat, staring at the tooth in his hand. Cletus pocketed his.

"Come on," he said. "Let's finish that beer, and get on over to the hospital to check on John Tyler. I want to hand these teeth off and get back home. I think some serious drinking is in order, and I got a bottle of Old Crow with my name on it."

"Might join you," Jasper said. "Not like I got a dinosaur to hunt…"

"And that," Cletus said, downing his beer, "is fine with me."

They drank in silence for a while, then left a tip on the table for Willow, hoping she wouldn't be too mad when she had to clean up after them, and headed out into the parking lot. The sun was almost down, lingering like a red eye over the trees in the distance.

"How long you reckon before that damn video is on the Internet?" Jasper asked. "I got a feelin' we might be goin' viral…"

"If I know Mack," Cletus said with a laugh, "it's already there. Bet we get some serious kudos for the special effects."

As he climbed into his truck and closed the door, he thought, just for a second, that he heard a loud, chirping whistle echoing over the fields. With a shiver he slammed the old Jeep into gear and spun gravel out of the parking lot. He hoped Mack and that damned bird stayed far away. Not that there was anything out there to answer it, but Cletus wasn't a man to take chances, and there was whiskey calling his name.

Want more O.C.L.T.?
Turn the page for a sample
from the first book in the series:

1

In a low bunker in the desert near the border of Jordan and the Dead Sea, a dozen men gathered. They arrived over a period of hours, none too close to behind the other to avoid any chance, even in this remote location, of being recognized together. They were not men given to solitary excursions, but each had left comrades and security behind in the interest of secrecy. They were robed, and their faces were covered against the whipping desert sand. Far above, the moon shone, pale and cloaked in clouds.

Salt clusters along the bank of the water glimmered oddly, almost glowing in the dim light. The water was as flat and lifeless as a sheet of glass. None of the twelve even glanced at it, though the last of them stopped and gazed directly across the surface toward Jerusalem. He stood there for only a moment, and then passed between the two squat, expressionless guards stationed outside the door. The two were associated with none of the twelve. They were carefully vetted mercenaries without affiliation. They didn't know who they guarded, or why, and they didn't care, as long as they were paid well, and on time.

Inside the building was a single long room. There was a small kitchenette, and a bathroom, relics of previous owners, but these were sealed. The room was centered by a rectangular table set very low to the ground. The twelve gathered around it. There was water, and tea, but for the most part the drinks were ignored. The room was lit by a single lamp on the table, as if those present weren't even comfortable knowing one another, let alone getting a good look.

When they were all seated, the man at the head of the table leaned back, glanced around at the others, and shook his head.

"We represent," he began, "an incredible gathering of power. The resources we command should be able to move mountains—with or without faith. We can, and have, bought kings and ambassadors."

"And for all of that," one of those to his left growled, "we have failed once again at the one task we must accomplish before all others."

There were mumbles of agreement all around. None of those gathered was happy, and each secretly blamed the others for their failure. They were not men accustomed to failure, or the denial of their desires. They dealt in blood, fortunes, and power. The one thing they shared—the one central binding power—was the passion of their faith. They were from a variety of nationalities, but theirs was a common enemy and a holy cause.

"Sometimes," the man who'd first spoken continued, "I feel as if we have lost our way. Allah places more obstacles in our way than he removes, and despite our unwavering loyalty, the Holy City is yet in the hands of the unclean. They have proclaimed themselves God's People to the world. What have we been proclaimed?"

"Killers," one of the others said.

"Terrorists," a third cut in. "They say that we care about nothing but the shedding of innocent blood. No matter that our beliefs are those of our fathers, and our father's fathers. No matter that the blasphemy of our most Holy City being handed by Western dogs to the unclean cuts us to the very soul."

He slammed his fist on the table. As sturdy as it was, the glasses and lamp jumped. Still, none of them rose. Their passion simmered, but it didn't boil over. Nothing that had been said was new. Theirs was an old hatred, and it burned slowly, but with great heat. It was fueled by frustration and the futility of their efforts.

"There must be a way," the first man spoke again. "Allah will show us that way."

The grim semi-silence of the gathering was broken by a peal of rich, feminine laughter. They spun as a single unit, drawing blades, and guns and diving back from the table with cries of surprise. They were leaders, but each of them had earned their position through years in the field. None of them was privileged by birth, and if they'd been compromised, every man of them would fight to the death.

There was no invading force. It was a lone woman, wrapped from head to foot in traditional Arab robes. Her head was swathed in a dark Hijab, covering all but her face. It was a remarkable face. Despite the dim light, her eyes glittered, and the grim line of her mouth was bent in a scornful frown. She stood with her arms crossed, glaring down at them as if she belonged—as if her presence did not break every law of their faith. As if all their security was so much dust in the desert.

"So," she said at last. "You have come to wallow in your defeat. How clever of you. How proud you must be. Allah would be pleased."

The first of the men back to his feet closed on her, his dagger raised.

The woman cocked her head and watched him, making no move to retreat.

"Who are you?" he asked. "How do you come here?"

"I came on the wind," she replied. "I come because you have called me. I come—because you have failed."

"You will not leave this place alive," the man said.

"I will," she said. "I will leave as I came, and I will leave with your promise, and your aid. You may call me Amunet."

The man closed on her quickly. He was not in the mood for idle chatter. He drove the dagger straight at her heart, but she only smiled. She spoke a single word—a word none of them heard clearly, and that none of them would have understood had they heard it.

The dagger shimmered and lost its rigidity. It coiled and turned back on itself, writhed and squirmed in the man's grip. He screamed, and tried to release it, but—now a serpent—it had coiled back around his wrist and moved up his arm toward his face. It was fast, and he staggered back, crashing into the table and falling across it, reaching to grab the snake behind its head and prevent it from reaching his face.

Two of the others ran to his side. One gripped the serpent behind its head, and the other dragged it free of his wrist. They held it—and then—with a cry of his own, the man gripping the neck cried out and backed away. His hand dripped blood where the sharp dagger blade had cut him. He stared at the wound in shock.

The dagger fell to the floor between them. The twelve turned and stared. Amunet gazed back at them, unperturbed.

"You will listen to me," she said. "You will help me, and I will help you. Though I am certain that my words are wasted, I will tell you this—there is nothing you can do to prevent it."

"Sorceress!" one of the men cried. "Allah protect us!"

Despite what they'd just witnessed, these were hard men. They were not going to be taken down by a simple illusion, and they were unused to being spoken to as lackeys—or for that matter, by women. Most of them were unaccustomed to a woman speaking to them at all if they had not addressed her first. The frustration of their recent endeavors, coupled with the ignominy of the situation was too much. They spread out and moved in quickly. They did not speak, they acted, but the woman, Amunet, did not back away. She raised both of her hands and spoke in clear, cutting tones.

Again, her words were lost to them. She seemed to speak in tongues, though now and then a phrase made the ghost of sense. The already dim light darkened, and there was a rising wail from outside the building. They ignored it. Before any of them could reach where the woman stood, the wailing was joined by twin screams.

They hesitated and turned toward the single door. There were no further screams, but the wail had grown to a roar, as if the desert had lifted up to sweep them away.

About the Author

David Niall Wilson has been writing and publishing horror, dark fantasy, and science fiction since the mid-eighties. An ordained minister, once President of the Horror Writer's Association and multiple recipient of the Bram Stoker Award, his novels include *The Second Veil, Hallowed Ground, Maelstrom, The Mote in Andrea's Eye, Deep Blue*, the Grails Covenant Trilogy, *Star Trek Voyager: Chrysalis, Except You Go Through Shadow, This is My Blood, Ancient Eyes, On the Third Day, The Orffyreus Wheel, Stargate Atlantis: Brimstone*, and the DeChance Chronicles. He has over 150 short stories published in anthologies, magazines, and five collections, the most recent of which were "Defining Moments" published in 2007 by WFC Award winning Sarob Press, and the currently available "Ennui & Other States of Madness," from Dark Regions Press. His work has appeared in and is due out in various anthologies and magazines. David lives and loves with Patricia Lee Macomber in the historic William R. White House in Hertford, NC with their children, Billy, Zach, Zane, and Katie, and occasionally their genius college daughter Stephanie. David is CEO and founder of Crossroad Press, a cutting edge digital publishing company specializing in electronic novels, collections, and non-fiction, as well as unabridged audiobooks.

Curious about other Crossroad Press books?
Stop by our site:
http://store.crossroadpress.com
We offer quality writing
in digital, audio, and print formats.

Enter the code FIRSTBOOK
to get 20% off your first order from our store!
Stop by today!

www.ingramcontent.com/pod-product-compliance
Lightning Source LLC
Chambersburg PA
CBHW060440180626
46817CB00007B/2914